2

D1733343

Also by Micheal Maxwell

Cole Sage Mysteries

Diamonds and Cole

Cellar of Cole

Helix of Cole

Cole Dust

Cole Shoot

Cole Fire

Heart of Cole

Cole Mine

Soul of Cole

Cole Cuts

Logan Connor Thrillers

Clean Cut Kid

East of the Jordan

Adam Dupree Mysteries

Dupree's Rebirth

Dupree's Reward

Dupree's Resolve

**Flynt and Steele Mysteries
(Written with Warren
Keith)**

Dead Beat

Dead Duck

Dead on Arrival

Dead Hand

Dead Ringer

Copyright © 2020 by Micheal Maxwell

All rights reserved. No part of this book may be reproduced in any form or by any means, electronic or mechanical, including photocopying, recording, or by any information storage and retrieval system, without permission in writing from the publisher.

ISBN: 9798698477716

COLE FIRE

MICHEAL MAXWELL

ONE

A tattered black and white MIA *Bring Them Home* flag snapped in the wind. Two feet away the Stars and Stripes were no longer red, white and blue but a sad, faded, bleed of color. Both flags bowed the thin wisp of rod they sat atop. Three feet below the symbols of pride and regret sat a man in a wheelchair. He faced the Taylor Street entrance of the Veterans Administration Hospital of San Francisco.

He wore the dress uniform of the United States Army. The deep blue was dusty on the shoulders and no longer fit like the youth it was issued to so many, many, years ago. His big belly kept the tarnished brass buttons from closing. A plaid blanket covered his lap, tightly tucked in at the sides and behind his thin lifeless legs.

Sitting in his lap was a manila envelope containing a letter stating his benefits no longer covered his *emotional* counseling. There was a nice paragraph about state and local options for treatment, and a short but curt sentence closed the letter with "consider this our last communication on this issue. Of course, all of your benefits for continued medical treatment are intact."

The letter's recipient had his head tilted back as he gazed motionless at the sky. In prayer perhaps, one

5

more of the myriad pleas made to the Almighty for help? He sat alone in the concrete and asphalt covered empty lot. The chain link fence around the lot partially blocked the view from the front doors of the hospital. It took a couple of hours for someone curious enough to walk across the grass and find the old warrior.

His cheap revolver lay on the ground next to him. Skull, hair, and brains streamed behind him like the tail of a comet. There was no longer a need for prayer or help from the Veteran's Administration. The Vietnam War had claimed another casualty. This one, however, would never be added to the tally.

* * *

"Wiltz."

"Mr. Wiltz, this is Tariq at the Taylor entrance."

"Hey, buddy, what's goin' on?"

"Nothing that wonderful. We have kind of a situation. I would count it a big favor if you could come on down." The security guard's voice was friendly but pleading.

"Alright. On my way."

Don Wiltz closed his office door and stopped at his secretary's desk on his way to the stairs.

"Something's up at the Taylor entrance. I'll be back in a few."

"Don't forget your eleven o'clock." Wiltz's secretary, Terri, was his greatest asset, and her reminders were not to go unheeded.

"I won't. Be right back." Don smiled.

Wiltz's mood was good for a Tuesday. By Friday, he would succumb to the feeling of hopelessness and despair that overshadowed every positive thing in his life. File by file, minute by minute, day by day, his job was killing him. Not in a physical sense, but emotionally, spiritually and psychologically. He was standing at the door of a very dark place.

The sight of police, ambulance and fire vehicles parked on Taylor Street as he rounded the stairwell and entered the lobby was a sure sign that the small blessings of this Tuesday morning were about to be crushed.

"Mr. Wiltz," Tariq said excitedly. "Thank you for comin' down."

Wiltz patted Tariq's shoulder and said, "What's all this?"

"One of ours, I think."

"What do you mean?"

"You better just go see. They kept asking me questions and I just don't know..."

"No problem. I'll go have a look."

Don Wiltz's aversion to lights and sirens bordered on phobia. Loud noises and bright lights were triggers he learned to live with. Years of counseling taught him the skills needed to center his thoughts and focus on his reflective exercises, to vanquish the panic.

The sounds of the first responders, who were staged but unneeded, were a mix of talking, shouting and radio squawks. Wiltz walked past the fire truck at the curb. Four police cars blocked the street and a coroner's van was pulled just inside the fence.

Two firemen stood at the gate of the construction fence, half-heartedly trying to loop the chain back around the gate in an attempt to hide the fact they cut the lock. As Don Wiltz approached, one of the firemen turned and said, "'Fraid you can't go in there, sir."

"What happened?"

"Appears to be a suicide."

"I'm a VA counselor. It was suggested the fellow might be one of ours."

"I'm afraid he's well beyond counseling. I don't guess it can hurt anything. Just wait until we walk off."

"Thanks," Wiltz offered. The firefighters made their way back to their truck and Wiltz pulled the chain and opened the gate.

As he made his way across the former building site, Wiltz self-consciously fumbled with the laminated name tag he wore around his neck. The lines of fresh sprouting weeds accented the cement, asphalt, and patch of bare ground as he made his way to the group standing fifty yards away. Nature reclaims, he thought as he kicked at the thin line of vegetation.

"Sorry, sir, you can't be in here," a uniformed policeman scolded as Wiltz approached the group scattered around the wheelchair.

"VA," Wiltz said, holding up his name badge, and kept walking as if he had every right to be there.

"You got all the shots you need?" A tall Asian man in a dark blue suit barked at a fat guy frantically snapping pictures.

"I guess so."

"Then you can take off."

"OK guys, he's all yours."

Two coroner's deputies rolled the waiting gurney closer to the man in the wheelchair.

"Wait. Please, just a moment," Wiltz said, stepping up to the group.

"And just who might you be?" the man in the suit asked gruffly.

"Don Wiltz, I'm a VA counselor," Wiltz gestured at the hospital across the street.

The man in the suit approached Wiltz with his hand outstretched. "Leonard Chin, San Francisco PD. Look, Mr. Wiltz, I don't know how you got in here but I'm afraid this gentleman no longer requires your help."

"I understand," Don said softly. "I just really wanted to see if he truly was one of ours. I just need a moment."

"OK guys, give him a second," Chin said to the coroner's deputies.

"Thank you, officer."

"Lieutenant," Chin said flatly.

Wiltz nodded and stepped up to the body in the wheelchair. He tried to not look at the deep purple bruising of the man's face. His eyes shifted to the brass name tag on the uniform. Baranski. Wiltz slowly looked up into the man's face. It was Charles Baranski, without a doubt. A wave of blurry lightheadedness came over Wiltz; the man was indeed "one of theirs".

"You know him?" Chin broke the silence.

"Yes, I'm afraid so."

"This could explain some things." Chin handed Wiltz the manila envelope from Baranski's lap.

It was a form letter. Don Wiltz had seen hundreds of them. More times than he could recall he tried to explain why men and women, mentally broken and scarred in the service of their country, no longer qualified for the slender thread of emotional support they clung to every hour of the day. The letter was not even dignified with a real signature, just a printed scribble at the bottom.

"It explains a lot," Wiltz said softly, handing back the envelope.

Without another word, Wiltz turned and started back toward the gate. Halfway there he threw up.

*   *   *

"Your eleven o'clock is here."

"I can't."

The door closed behind Don Wiltz. He didn't turn the light on. He walked to the window and closed the blinds. It wasn't dark but it was close. For a long moment, he stood in the center of his office facing his desk. He repeatedly ran his tongue back and forth across his upper lip. Both of his fists were clenched tightly and softly pounded against the side of his hips.

To make the darkness complete, Don Wiltz squeezed his eyes tightly closed. He was in the dark place. He stepped over the threshold into his inner self, his deepest fears, regrets, and the long-buried trauma of war. He dropped to a squatting position and crossed his arms over his head. Silently he rolled onto his back, then to his side. Don Wiltz was frozen. He couldn't move. It felt good. The darkness and hard carpeted floor were a solid place to be, but there was another way, a way to feel even better, safer, protected.

It took his every muscle, every sinew, all his will, but he began to shift his weight, rolling first to his shoulders, then his hips. Wiltz wriggled his way around his desk. He pushed his chair back with his head and neck. He rolled and scooted until he was under his desk, his back resting against the front panel. Using both hands he covered his eyes.

The bloody purple flesh that was Charlie Baranski's face projected in the dark. The image would not fade. He saw the fragile, wounded man across his desk turn into a bruised, skull-less mask, then back again. Charlie was eaten by the war machine, fodder for the guns of meaningless enemies. Charlie was Vietnam, Iraq, Afghanistan, Korea, and Bosnia. Charlie was the client list that never got smaller, just more and more every day, young men, young women who were never able to return, unable to bathe their souls in the balm of home, family, wives, lovers, friends. The stain of blood and terror tattooed their very being. Some were now past retirement age, some middle-aged, and some in their prime years of life, but all imprisoned in the hell of war.

Little did they know that the shrapnel of fear they carried was also embedded deep within the man they looked to for words, for truth, for salvation. The man who the government paid to help piece their lives back together again was just as fragile, just as damaged as they were. His scars were just covered deeper by decades of calluses.

As Wiltz lay in the dark under his desk, rocking back and forth and humming *Gimme Shelter*, he fell asleep.

The knock on the door was not the light tap of a gentle interruption. It was a demand, an order to pay attention.

"Don? You all right?" Terri's voice cut through the door as if it wasn't there.

Wiltz scrambled to get to his chair.

"Don?" This time the voice was accompanied by a shaft of brilliant white light cutting through the cool dark comfort of his office.

"Yeah, yeah, fine. I have a headache, that's all." Wiltz lied.

"It's four o'clock. I've got a doctor appointment, remember?"

"Yes, just close the door, the light is killing me," Wiltz demanded.

"You want something for it? Tylenol, aspirin?" Terri's tone softened.

"No, it wouldn't work. Thank you. Sorry I snapped at you."

"You should go home. I'll let the voicemail take the calls. I gotta roll. You go home. Hope you feel better," Terri offered as she let the door close easily behind her.

Wiltz sat in the dark for a few minutes longer. Finally, he went to the window and slowly cracked the blinds. Little by little, he let the dim late afternoon light wash into his office from the shady side of the building. He stood watching the wind blow the trees in the distance. Thirty years of kind words, encouragement and meaningless blather. That is what his life represented.

"We can no longer cover your emotional counseling," Wiltz said mockingly into the half-lit office.

With his hands driven deep into his pockets, Don Wiltz left his department. Again, he took the stairs. Thankfully, he made no human contact on his way out of the building.

He didn't want to, he tried hard not to, but he just had to look across the street at where Charlie Baranski was found. The asphalt and concrete were bare, awaiting the start of new construction. He frantically searched for police tape or something that would mark the spot, then he saw the dark stain of Charlie's last act. Wiltz threw his arm over his eyes and walked on. The transit bus was pulling up as Wiltz approached the corner of Taylor and Damen. He ran the last few yards to the bus.

Just three more stops for Wiltz on his way home. Six people got off and three got on. This time Don Wiltz noticed something different. An Asian couple, laughing and giggling, got on the bus and sat across the aisle and one seat ahead of him. The girl was pretty, and the young man was neatly groomed. They were both well dressed and obviously in love.

Wiltz watched them chat as the bus rolled along. He was no longer in San Francisco. Her shiny black hair and brown skin were a Saigon photograph come to life. Don Wiltz owned albums full of similar pictures. Bar girls, shop girls, pretty Southeast Asian beauties. What was she doing here?

At the next stop, Wiltz moved to the seat in front of the couple. He waited for the bus to get up to speed before he turned around.

"He died for you!" Wiltz said to the couple.

"I'm sorry?" The young man replied politely.

"He died for you," Wiltz repeated.

"We have our own religion, thank you for sharing." The young man was polite but firm.

"Charles Baranski."

"Nice to meet you."

"No, Charles Baranski died so you could be here; Ride this bus, breathe this free air in San Francisco."

"Then we're grateful. Look, we just want to ride in peace. We don't want any problems."

The speaker overhead crackled and the harsh voice of the driver bellowed out a warning question, "Is there a problem back there?"

Wiltz spun around in his seat. He didn't see the young man wave an OK sign to the driver. The couple shrugged and grinned at each other. Just another San Francisco crazy, they whispered. Two stops later the young man bid his girlfriend good-bye and hopped off the bus.

As if coming out of a dream, Wiltz opened his eyes and realized the bus was pulling away from his stop. He must have dozed off. Somehow it didn't matter. He could have jumped up and probably been able to get off. He just sat and watched as the bus rolled along. Out the window were signs, stores, and street names Don wasn't familiar with. He was back in San Francisco. The memories of Saigon faded and were replaced by an uneasy feeling of concern. He needed to get home. He must get off the bus and get turned around. In another moment, he thought.

Just the other side of Ainslie the bus pulled over. It was a busy stop, people moving in and out, jostling bags, backpacks, and strollers. He watched the line shorten, then he saw her. The girl behind him got off the bus and was walking away. Wiltz jumped to his feet and pressed his way through the crowd to the rear exit.

The harsh glare of the late afternoon sun was turning to the muted shades of dusk. A group of people were making their way along the sidewalk ahead of him. In the center of the group, the young Southeast Asian woman walked alone. Wiltz recognized her black leather jacket, and the bright red purse she clutched so tightly when he tried to talk to them. Without taking his eyes from her, Wiltz began to follow.

All around him the signs of Pho shops and Vietnamese markets began to light up. One by one, on both sides of the street, the dull colors of twilight were vanquished in the reds and blues of neon signs. Wiltz looked around him. The lettering on the shop windows took him back to Vietnam. The people passing were no longer the predominantly white majority where he lived, but almost all Southeast Asian.

Wiltz floated just between the cracking world of the in-control, self-assured VA counselor and a panicked twenty-year-old soldier wandering the streets and alleys of 1973 Saigon. One moment the sixty-one-year-old was questioning why he was following a young girl through Little Saigon; the next, he was a soldier on the lookout for his next "hot date."

"These are the enemy," he said to no one. "You need to find the other guys. Get back to the group. Never wander off alone. That's what the sergeant said."

The bustle of early evening was a distraction, and when Wiltz refocused and looked ahead, the girl was gone. He glanced up both sides of the street. The sidewalks were busy, but not so much he couldn't have spotted her. Where did she go?

Walking slowly, almost cat-like, Wiltz looked in each shop and business he passed. Once he saw his reflection in the window of a restaurant and was confused at his image. His search turned up nothing. In a lucid moment, he asked himself what it mattered. He didn't know the girl. It was then that the voice came to him.

"She's VC."

* * *

The first time he heard the voice, he shook it off and walked on. The second time he heard it, he realized it was Charles Baranski.

"It's her fault, Don," the voice said.

As Wiltz stopped in front of *Happy Three Nails*, he saw the girl. She was taking off her jacket and hanging it on a coat rack behind the reception desk.

"This place is crawling with Gooks," the voice said.

"Don't use that word. It's racist." Wiltz said aloud.

"Gook, Gook, Gook!" Charlie's voice screamed in his head. "I bet this is where the tunnels start."

"Stop. There is nothing I can do." Wiltz answered.

"Really? This is how heroes are made. Medals are won. Legends are born." Charlie Baranski was as frightening as he was beguiling.

"What do we do?"

"Get back to the barracks; come up with a plan of attack. Come back under cover of darkness." Charlie chuckled, then coughed in his raspy Marlboro hack.

Don Wiltz stepped back from the window. He watched from the shadows as the girl took her place behind a nail station. She unlocked the drawer and took out a set of files, clippers, and acrylic nails. She spun around in her chair and took inventory of the polish on the wall behind her.

* * *

The two blocks back to the bus stop took less than three minutes. Wiltz ran as if his life depended on it. He paced and mumbled while he waited for the bus. Within thirty minutes he was unlocking the door to his apartment.

Wiltz ignored the blinking yellow light on his telephone, so he didn't know Terri called to check up on him. He was never one to pick up on signals; an odd thing for a counselor trained to find the root of people's problems. Terri constantly gave out signals. It was obvious to everyone in the department that she was more than willing to continue their day together after hours. The presents on his birthday, Christmas, Easter, Veteran's Day, Boss's Day, even a heart-shaped box of chocolates on Valentine's Day were just "nice gestures" in Wiltz's myopic view of his work-place.

Several of the men in the Mental Health De-partment, both married and single, were falling all over themselves for the pretty widowed secretary who sat outside Wiltz's door. They were all wasting their time because Terri only had eyes for her boss.

The sound of his keys dropping into the glass bowl on the counter sounded like glass beads in a doorway. He was back in Saigon. He stood in the middle of his small living room and slowly turned around. Round and round. The sounds of mortars in the distance made his breathing quicken. As he be-came more aware of the pulsing blood in his temples the mortar shells grew closer.

"They're moving into the city." Charlie's voice cut through the half-lit townhouse.

"The tunnels." Tunnels are running under your girlfriend's shop."

"She's not my girlfriend," Wiltz snapped.

"We gotta take them out. Burn them out."

"I need to tell someone."

"No!" Charlie shouted. "We're doing this ourselves. Then we take the credit, get the glory, and get the medal."

"But how?"

"Napalm," Charlie whispered.

"Napalm?"

"Like we made in Nam."

"I never..."

"Yes, you did." Charlie laughed hoarsely. "Hurry up. We'll go back at midnight."

Wiltz went to the refrigerator. He removed the two-liter bottle of orange soda and poured what was left of it into three glasses. In the cupboard under the stove, he pulled out the stack of Styrofoam takeaway cartons from the Chinese restaurant. He never wasted anything: they were washed, cleaned and stacked. But this was the first time he'd ever used one.

Bit by bit, he tore a Styro carton into little thumbnail-sized pieces and dropped them into the soda bottle. A third of the way full and two-and-a-half cartons later, he stopped.

The white cap screwed down tight, he set the bottle on the counter. In the upstairs bedroom where no one ever slept, Wiltz flipped through the old shirts, sweaters, and jackets until he spotted the army green field jacket. He stared for a moment at the patch with WILTZ stitched on the chest. He slipped the jacket on and went into the bathroom.

His hands trembled as he fumbled with the zipper. Zipping it all the way to the neck, Wiltz stared into the mirror, pleased that it still fit. Careful to turn the light off as he left the room, Wiltz returned to the kitchen, grabbed the soda bottle and his car keys from the glass bowl on the counter.

*   *   *

The silver Mazda in the one-car garage was rarely driven. He preferred the bus. It forced him to walk to the stop, and then to his office. The last time registration came due from the state he pondered the idea of letting it lapse. In the corner of the tiny space was a red gas can. Even though he only drove to out of town meetings, he kept the gas can full and ready to go. It sat on the garage floor for fear it would cause a fire if he left it in the trunk, but when he left town it was always in the trunk.

Reversing the nozzle lid, Wiltz carefully filled the soda bottle with gasoline. Gently rolling the bottle and tilting it end to end, he watched the Styrofoam pieces begin to dissolve into a translucent gel. Satisfied his mixture was complete, he unlocked the trunk and gently laid the bottle on the canvas emergency bag. He made sure it was cradled atop the bag so it wouldn't roll around as he drove. He set the gas can tight against it.

Four hours later, he returned to the garage. The drive back to *Happy 3* took less time than Wiltz thought. The street was empty, and the shops were all closed. He circled the block twice. Pulling into the alley, Wiltz turned his headlights off and used only his parking lights. The alley behind the row of shops was dark except for a lone light bulb burning over an unmarked back door. In his parking lights, he saw H3N sprayed across a grey steel door in pink paint. He stopped and got out.

Moving quickly, Wiltz popped the trunk and lifted out the soda bottle. He shook it hard several times. The mixture was perfect. At the bottom of the nail shop's door was a thick and badly worn rubber weather strip. He fished around in his emergency bag and found a large, flat tip screwdriver.

The screws on the weatherstrip were rusty and gave way easily as Wiltz repeatedly jammed the screwdriver behind the strip and jerked it away from the door. It only took a minute to remove the strip and expose the nearly inch-wide gap at the bottom of the door.

He gave the bottle one more, good hard shake and removed the cap. He tried to pour the homemade napalm under the door, but as much spilled outside the building as in. Glancing around, he spotted a pizza box in the garbage-strewn alley a few feet away. He unfolded the box and slipped it partway under the door. Wiltz gently poured his mixture down the greasy lid of the box. Like water down a storm drain, the "dragon fire" ran under the door.

As the bottle emptied, Wiltz shoved the box under the door and wedged the bottle into the gap. He reached in the large pocket of his jacket and took out the box of wooden matches from the kitchen.

"Nice work," the voice in his head said proudly.

"Are you happy, Charlie?"

"I am proud," Charlie replied.

Don Wiltz snapped to attention. Just as in days long gone, he saluted, then struck a match. The ground around the door exploded in flames and Wiltz jumped back and hit hard against the car.

He got in and slowly pulled away. Rounding the corner, he drove past Happy 3 Nails, pausing just long enough to see a smoky, orange glow behind the hanging beads in the doorway leading into the back room.

"Good job, soldier." Charlie's voice was as clear and strong as when he sat across Wiltz' desk.

TWO

"Higher, Grandpa, higher!" Jenny squealed with delight as she watched the kaleidoscope colors of the Rabbit kite rise higher and higher into the azure blue April sky.

Cole let the string unspool. The kite pulled against the line as it lifted and swayed high above San Francisco Bay. He watched it spinning and diving, only to rise higher and higher and farther out, over the white-capped water. The little girl and her grandpa were so focused they were unaware of the dozens and dozens of fellow kite pilots that surrounded them.

"Look this way!" Kelly called out. With her camera poised to catch "Team 408" attempting to win the "Build Your Own" kite competition, she pleaded with her subjects to pose. "Come on, you guys, just one picture!" Kelly's voice was partially lost on the wind but completely lost to the concentration of Team 408.

A green and orange Tiger kite swerved and banged against Cole and Jenny's Kaleidoscope Rabbit. In an instant, the Tiger was plummeting to earth in a nose-first tailspin. As it spun earthward it draped over the strings of a large white Angel kite and a silver and black Oakland Raiders Rocket kite. To the accompaniment of screams and tears, the trio of sticks and colorful tissue fell into the bay.

As parents tried to comfort their pint-sized teammates, Cole continued to coax the Rabbit kite higher and higher into the blue.

"Grandma, grandma! Look, look!" Jenny pointed skyward, one hand blocking her eyes from the sun.

Kelly snapped pictures and laughed at the sight of Cole dancing and stumbling his way around the other contestants. One by one, kites rose and fluttered in the strong April breezes. More strings tangled and the hopes of other kite lovers were dashed on the rocks and water of San Francisco Bay.

Above the cheers and cries of the kite builders, the sound of Lee Dorsey, singing *Working in a Coal Mine* on Cole's phone suddenly cut through the noise. "Goin' down, down, down..."

"Kelly! Help!" Cole yelled into the wind as Lee Dorsey moaned "Lord how long can this go on!"

Cole was playing hooky from work to meet his granddaughter and her paternal grandmother at the Kite Festival. The sound of *Working in a Coal Mine* meant that Chuck Waddell, his boss and feature editor of the *San Francisco Chronicle*, was calling.

"Here, give me that," Kelly said, taking the spool of string in one hand, and sliding the other under the lead line to the kite.

"Hello, Chuck?" Cole called into the phone trying to shield it from the wind.

"Where are you?" Waddell replied.

"Crissy Field! Kite Festival today."

"I need you to get on a story right away. Jesse Monday is dead."

"What? How?" Suddenly Cole felt as if he were standing all alone on the meadow.

"Shot," Waddell said solemnly. "Here's the thing though, his body has disappeared."

"What do you mean, disappeared?" Cole asked, not fully taking in the news.

"It's gone. They took him to the morgue, then the funeral home. And he's disappeared."

"That's crazy," said Cole, still not believing what he was hearing.

"I need you to get the jump on this. I worked up a website piece—well, Rob did, but this is our story. We've been on him since day one. We need to do a bio/obit piece, too. Can you handle both?"

"I'll be right in," Cole said.

Without realizing it, Cole wandered several yards from where Kelly and Jenny were. He ran his hand through his hair and sighed.

"What's the matter? You look like somebody died," Kelly said as Cole rejoined them.

"They did," Cole answered.

"Who?" Kelly asked, fumbling with the kite spool.

"Grandma! The kite!" Jenny screamed.

Kelly turned back to the kite just in time to see it flipping through the air on its way to a watery demise. Cole grabbed the spool and string from her and yanked back hard. The kite seemed to stop in mid-flight and right itself. Slowly it began to climb. Cole took a deep breath and looked at Kelly, who stood with both hands over her mouth, staring up at the Kaleidoscope Rabbit.

"I have to get to the paper. Jesse Monday has been killed. To make matters worse, the body has disappeared."

"Jesse Monday, the cult guy?"

"That's the one. I'll meet you back at your place later." Cole turned and knelt down next to Jenny. "Grandpa has to go back to work. I'll meet you at Grandma's later, OK?"

The little girl threw her arms around Cole's neck and gave him a tight squeeze. "Grandma will crash the kite, you know," Jenny whispered.

"Maybe, but we won't tease her about it, OK?" Cole whispered back.

"It's OK if she crashes. We just won't win, that's all." Jenny let go of Cole and turned and watched Kelly struggle with the kite. She shook her head, resigned to the fact that, for her, the competition was over.

The inside of the car was warm from the bright spring sun and the heat felt good on Cole's back as he settled into the seat. He was parked in the back corner of the lot behind the Palace of Fine Arts, and as he pulled out onto the street he snapped off the radio and tried to recall his first memories of Jesse Monday. Cole was new to San Francisco then, having just moved from Chicago. Jesse was holding a kind of open-air meeting in Golden Gate Park.

As he made his way across town to the *Chronicle,* Cole remembered several years ago Chuck Waddell sending him to check out the "Jesse Movement."

"What do you want me to get from it?" Cole asked.

"The truth," was all Waddell replied.

"The truth?" Cole asked.

"Look, what I want is for you to see this guy first-hand, and to call it like you see it." Cole thought Chuck Waddell's tone was strained and a little curt.

"All right," Cole began. "I'll check it out."

As he drove he remembered the day he went to Golden Gate Park, his first encounter with Jesse Monday. He saw streams of people making their way toward the big meadow. Cole parked and joined the procession. The crowd was made up mostly of young people in their twenties, some alone, some were couples holding hands, and some were pushing baby strollers. They were all colors, shapes, and sizes, but from their dress, most were not what anyone would call upwardly mobile.

"Say, where is everybody going?" Cole asked a tall blonde couple.

"To see Jesse!" they beamed.

"Jesse?" Cole acted dumb.

"Jesse Monday. You haven't heard of him?" the young man said, adjusting his backpack.

"No, is he a singer or something?" Cole asked.

"He's a teacher, a wonderful spiritual teacher."

"He's changing the world one person at a time. You really should come along and hear him," the pretty, freckled, but too thin young woman's tone was friendly, happy, yet almost pleading.

"Sounds like I should. I'm not really religious, though," Cole said, hoping to draw out a response.

"He's just the truth."

There it was again, "the truth." A strange shudder came over Cole. Did Chuck mean it the way this young couple used it? Cole dismissed the thought as quickly as it came. Yet it was a strange choice of words. Almost slogan-like in its simplicity, and yet it was the hook that they used to try to pull Cole into attending the event.

He struck up the same kind of conversation with a half-dozen other people as he made his way along the crowd. A more than a little overweight Hispanic guy, with bad acne and drinking a bottle of Snapple tea, wasn't sure why he was there but was told that Jesse had things to say that helped his neighbor. A Chinese girl in a pale gray warm-up suit said she was a cancer survivor and credited Jesse with giving her the courage to not give up when she was at her lowest. All the people Cole talked to were drawn to Jesse Monday for their own reasons. None were idle curiosity seekers, and none of them appeared to be looking for personal gain.

The most fascinating person Cole talked to, though, was a black woman in a nun's habit. "Why are you here, Sister?" Cole inquired.

"The message here is one of hope, love, and truth. I have heard from several who come to our women's shelter that Jesse has healed the sick. I want to see if he is a modern-day prophet—or perhaps a saint."

"Does the church approve of Jesse Monday?" Cole asked.

"This isn't about the church," she answered. Cole thought it a very strange response from a Bride of Christ, but before he could pursue this line of questioning, they came to the edge of the meadow and the nun disappeared into the crowd.

Across the meadow, a crowd of about two thousand was gathered. Blankets and lawn chairs were spread out in a half moon and faced a wooden platform brought in to provide a makeshift stage. A few feet from the stage stood a man with an acoustic guitar that paced back and forth with his head down and his hands in his pockets. Behind him, Cole saw a line of at least four or five hundred people making their way to the meadow.

Cole rounded the crowd to the far right side and spotted a seat on the grass about fifty feet from the stage. A small woman with bone-thin features and short bobbed hair turned and smiled at Cole.

"Hessee will heal my 'earing today," The woman said in the unmistakable nasal tones of a person who learned to speak without hearing. In both of her ears were large flesh-colored hearing aids.

Cole looked straight at her and asked slowly and clearly, "Is that true?"

"I believe. Thaz all tha' matters. Hessee says, 'Believe an' receive'."

"I hope you will." Cole smiled and nodded at the woman.

The man with the guitar mounted the stage. He was rather small, with a spikey hair-do. His clothes seemed a bit young for him, for when you looked closely, his face was lined and weathered, and his features were those of someone much closer to fifty, than the twenty-something he was trying to project. With a broad windmill sweep of his arm, the guitarist hit a chord on the guitar.

"Welcome! Let us raise our voice in song!"

The crowd seemed to leap to their feet as if one huge being. Cole didn't recognize the words of the first song but the melody was plainly lifted from the chorus of John Lennon's *Give Peace a Chance*.

"If we believe, it shall be done. We can make a difference in everyone." The crowd sang along, some waving their hands above their heads and some just gently swaying to the music. The refrain was repeated time and again, the volume rising and falling as the guitarist directed and led the group.

After three more reworked familiar rock and folk songs, the song leader waved his hand and yelled, "That was great! Find the truth!" Waving to the crowd again, he left the stage.

Cole took his time being seated and watched the crowd as they turned and settled on the grass. When he looked back at the small stage, to his amazement, a man stood where seconds before the guitarist had been.

Dressed in a pair of blue jeans and a simple work shirt, he could have been any of a million working guys you could pass on the street or stand in line with at McDonald's, never even noticing them. His hair was a shaggy medium brown, cut in no particular style, and his face was that of the average white man, with a short brown beard your see on any street. He was neither handsome nor was he unattractive. He was a face in the crowd. He stood about five foot ten, was of medium build, had the look of someone who enjoyed the outdoors and spent a lot of time in the sunshine. The only striking feature of this man was his eyes.

Even from where Cole sat he could see they were blue. Not just blue, though; they could only be described as a piercing, nearly luminescent blue. As he looked across the silent crowd he seemed to see every face. When he turned toward the side where Cole sat, he could have sworn that they looked eye to eye. Cole didn't like the feeling of looking into the eyes of this man.

"It is a day like no other. And we will never see its likes again," he began. In the distance you could hear the low hum of traffic, a horn honked and a bus revved its engine, but the crowd was silent. Cole wondered for a second if they were even breathing. "It is said that the end of days will come upon us like a thief in the night. I am here to tell you that thief is in the driveway. The wickedness and evil that surrounds this city are not unique. The whole world over, people have turned away from Truth and has chosen their own path." He spoke with a calm authority. Without straining or shouting, his voice carried across the crowd. This was Jesse Monday, the man Cole was sent to see.

His message was pretty simple. Find the Truth, the end is near. Just like the thousands of cartoons over the years in the *New Yorker* magazine, yet he was not a longhaired prophet of doom in a long white robe. He was an ordinary-looking guy with a simple style and delivery.

"There was a man who lived in a house by the side of a road that ran along a canyon. The only way to the beautiful valley beyond the canyon was across the walkway he built in front of his house. In front of his house near the road was a pile of round river rocks. The man who lived in the house was old and didn't like talking to the people who passed by. He spent his days just sweeping the walkway, clearing the trash and repairing the boards that would wear out along the walkway.

"He thinks he's better than us," people would grumble as they passed the house. The Hermit just ignored them and that made them grumble all the more.

One day a man picked up one of the river rocks and threw it at the Hermit's house. It hit the side and rolled away. The Hermit didn't pay it any mind. He just went about his business. A while later, another man picked up one of the rocks and hurled it at the house. This went on for several days. The pile of rocks was getting smaller as each day passed."

Jesse paused and stepped down from the platform.

"Finally the pile of rocks had all but disappeared." Jesse bent down and picked up a small stone that was in the grass and turned it in his hand. "The Hermit used all the rocks that were thrown at his house to make a lovely flower bed all around the front of his house." He turned and hopped back up on the small wooden stage.

"A large, angry man came along, who threw a rock almost every day at the Hermit's house and picked up the last rock. "Hey, Hermit!" the man yelled. "Here's your last rock!" and with that, he threw it with all his might at the house. Just then the walkway below his feet began to shudder. The angry man removed the last of the stones piled up to counterbalance the weight of the walkway. The walkway fell into the canyon, along with the man." Jesse tossed the small stone in his hand back onto the grass.

"After that, the people would come to the far edge where the walkway used to be and call at the house, "Hey, Hermit!" Jesse cupped his hands over his mouth and pretended to yell. 'Please, rebuild the walkway!' But you know, the Hermit couldn't hear them."

Jesse stood perfectly still and looked out at the crowd. Then he said, "Those rocks are just like the good, true things in the world. They balanced out the path in our lives, but all too many of you chose to just throw them away. Just like the Hermit, the Truth we find can help to build things of beauty. You must learn to lead a balanced life. Let the stones of righteousness outweigh the evil in the world before it destroys your path to Truth. Soon all the rocks will be gone in this world. There will be no one to hear our cries for help. Truth will be gone forever. It is up to each of us to reach out and share the Truth."

After an hour of similar stories, Jesse left the platform, and as the crowd stood to sing another song with the guitarist, he disappeared into the trees. The crowd stayed for a while just talking and laughing, but within a few minutes, they picked up their blankets and lawn chairs and drifted back the way they came.

Cole watched as three men in jeans and work boots came and knocked down the platform, and each carrying a piece of the wood and then slipped into the trees. As the crowd drifted away, Cole remembered the deaf girl. He scanned the crowd but she was gone. *Funny he should think of her*, he thought.

* * *

Cole's thoughts were interrupted by the blaring horn of a graffiti-covered seafood truck that nearly hit him as it came barreling out of the alley to his right. Almost three years passed since he first saw Jesse in Golden Gate Park. He'd only been in San Francisco a couple of weeks and never heard of the scruffy street preacher that was now praised by as many people as those who reviled him.

As he made his way to his office, Cole was struck by the solemn mood in the building. Small clusters of people stood around in hushed conversations. He passed several women in their cubicles who were weeping. Three people stopped Cole to ask if he'd heard the news. At his office door, he met Chuck Waddell who was putting a note on his door.

"That was quick," Chuck said retrieving the note from the rack on the door. "I was just leaving this." He handed Cole the envelope. "I jotted down a few things I want to make sure you cover. I know, I know, you don't need me to tell you how to write an article. It is just that, well, I have some mixed feelings about Jesse Monday and..."

"Your e-mail not working? What's going on, Chuck?"

"Just before Chris, before he..." Chuck stopped short. The memory of his partner, lover, and best friend being killed was something that Chuck still couldn't fully deal with. "He'd begun following Jesse, I mean he was interested in, hell, I don't know what I mean. I just want the truth, Cole, you know what I mean, the truth?"

"You mean was Jesse Monday a prophet, or the second coming, or something besides a street preacher? Come on, Chuck, I know a lot of people put a lot of stock in this guy, but he was what he was, right?"

"I don't know. Chris thought he was something very special. Said he did miracles, healed people. I know it sounds stupid but he said he even raised the dead."

"And now he's dead," Cole said flatly.

"And now he's dead," Chuck looked small and pale as he spoke of his murdered partner. "But Chris said that he would come back, you know, resurrect, just like Jesus. If there is something to all this, if there is a chance that Chris is in heaven or someplace better than this life, I want to know if we can be together. I mean..." Chuck took a deep breath. "You think I'm a fool, don't you?" Chuck's voice cracked as he laced his fingers behind his head and looked up at the ceiling.

"No, I think grief takes a lot longer than you realize." Cole reached over and patted his old friend on the shoulder. "We all live with the hope that we'll be with those we love in the hereafter. Death would be too painful to deal with without that hope. Monday was a great teacher and did a lot of good for this community, but I'm not sure how much divinity I would hang on him.

"Look, I'll poke around into this whole thing and see what I can find out. We have a lot of material on Jesse Monday and his followers. Let's see what I can put together."

"That's all I ask." Chuck turned and made his way to the elevators without another word.

Cole flopped down in his desk chair and rubbed his face with both hands. In all his years as a reporter and columnist, he never faced a story that challenged his sense of structure more than this one. Chuck didn't care about the story, at least not on the surface. He wanted answers, universal answers; Cole was not the one to give them. Jesse Monday was a hot button for hundreds, maybe thousands, since he appeared on the scene three years ago. The fundamental beliefs and understanding of religion and how it was supposed to work were turned upside-down by a soft-spoken street preacher and his rag-tag army of followers. Not since the heyday of the hippies had San Francisco seen so much attention paid to the outermost fringe elements of the city.

Cole's spiritual life was dormant, dead, or dysfunctional for years. There were no words to really explain his lack of interest or need for things spiritual. Four years ago when he was reunited with Ellie, the need for prayer was thrust upon him. He lost her for over twenty years. Alone, drifting and consumed by his work, he lived in the shadow of finding her again until he was bogged down in a hopeless mire of depression and apathy. Their reunion was short-lived and he lost her again, only this time to a terminal illness.

He cried out to God for Ellie's healing, her forgiveness, and finally in the soul-wrenching pain of losing her. His answer was discovering that they had a daughter, Erin. The faith that she shares with her husband Ben, and the way they are raising their daughter, showed Cole that a life of faith was not one of hypocrisy or charlatanism, but a strong foundation that they built their lives on.

Then there was Kelly Mitchell. Her faith was as natural and as much of her being as her smile and her wit. Her faith was something she was, not something she did. The strange circle that spins around his life didn't prepare Cole for his newly discovered daughter being married to the son of the woman he would fall so deeply and truly in love with. Should they ever marry, the twisted branches of the family tree would surely confound future generations of genealogists.

Cole had no use for long-winded preachers or show biz production church services. He went, on occasion, to the same church that his friend and baseball buddy Cornell attended with his family. The stomp and shout exuberance of the congregation gave him hope for a heaven filled with people just like them.

The difference between the big church in the Mission District, and the small fellowship in the newly remodeled warehouse in Sausalito that Kelly attended was in in the racial lines the congregants broke down into. Where the black church boasted a choir of at least a hundred in purple robes with no need of amplification, Kelly's church's worship team of old guitar-playing hippies that sang a combination of old hymns and new repetitive choruses and were miked, equalized, and pushed through a dozen JBL house monitors.

Cole often joked when confronted with the dogma of an overbearing proselytizer that he only believed two things, "First, there is a God, and second, you're not him." That, in a nutshell, was what bothered him most about Jesse Monday. Cole was sure if and when he met God, The Almighty would not find it necessary to tell everyone who he was. Moreover, in the history of mankind, and to the best of his knowledge, Cole was pretty certain that God never needed to hire a P.R. team.

It took Cole almost a minute to find his business card file in the chaos of his desk. He flipped through cards old and new until he found Carter Washington. He punched in the number and waited.

Four rings and a very mechanical woman's voice said, "Carter Washington's office, how may I help?"

"Cole Sage calling, is Mr. Washington in?"

"Who are you with?"

"I'm by myself," Cole said dryly.

"I see. Please hold."

"Cole, is that you?"

"Hey, Carter, how's it goin'?"

"Great! Good to hear from you. I know this isn't social—what am I going to do for you?" Carter laughed.

"Well, you did say if I ever needed anything... This is a little thing, I think," Cole began. "You've probably heard Jesse Monday was shot."

"I did." Carter Washington assumed his full FBI voice and Cole could just see him suddenly sitting ramrod straight in his chair.

"I need any and everything you can give me on him."

"Look, Cole, I know that you understand how things work..." Washington's voice trailed off.

"So, I won't expect a fax or a FedEx package in the next day or two."

"I didn't say that. Hold on." After a series of clicks and hums, the line went dead.

Cole shrugged, put the phone back on its base, closed the card file and exhaled. A moment later his cell phone rang.

"Hello."

"Had to get a clear line, you never know who's listening these days. What the hell you want stuff on Monday for? Never mind. Look, this guy has stirred up a lot of folks back here. What's your angle on this?"

"The boss wants a feature slash bio piece."

"You're not buying into this 'second coming' nonsense are you?"

"Who's putting that out?" Cole saw the conversation going in a whole different direction than he anticipated.

"We've had people on the ground in California for three years tracking this guy. I'll send you everything I can. If you turn up anything though, I would appreciate getting a copy. The sooner we close this thing the better. Our department is being flooded with calls from every Bible Belt Senator and Congressman you can imagine, plus a few northern liberals that would surprise you.

"Your Mr. Monday is seen as a real threat to the Christian community in this country. Throw in a Rabbi or two and you have the majority of religious folks in America none too happy with your crackpot in California claiming to be God, Jesus or whoever, returning to Earth, or whatever."

"I figured you guys would have an eye on him but I never imagined he was known outside the Bay Area."

"The fear was that the Jesse for Governor Movement would swell into a Jesse for President Movement. The last thing the boys on the Hill want is some goofy third-party candidate throwing off the delicate balance of our beloved two-party system." Washington laughed.

"That's pretty radical talk for a Bureau department head."

"More cynical than radical, I'm afraid. But God help us if this guy should somehow 'resurrect.' That would really throw a monkey wrench into the whole mess," Washington said with a sarcastic sting to his tone.

The old friends chatted and swapped stories for another fifteen minutes. The conversation started to lag and Cole promised copies of whatever he turned up on Jesse Monday. Carter Washington said he would get an overnight package out before the end of the day. Cole heard the ringing of Washington's other line and ended the call.

The next call Cole made was to Randy Callen. Without a doubt, Callen was the best researcher Cole ever worked with. He possessed the uncanny ability to ferret out information on the net almost before Cole could finish explaining what he wanted. Randy's willingness to tap dance around legalities, and his willingness to slither in and out of places he didn't belong, endeared him to Cole long ago.

"Hey, how's my favorite cellar dweller?"

"I'll have you know we of the subterranean persuasion refer to our non-windowed abode as the basement, thank you very much."

"I need everything you can get your hands on about Jesse Monday."

"Already on it. I figured somebody would be doing the obit. Why you, Cole?" Callen asked with a faint hint of surprise.

"Waddell wants a feature that will double as an obit."

"How deep do you want me to go?"

"Where ever it leads you, Cole answered.

The fact that Randy Callen could and would be led into the files of state, Federal and private agencies without their knowledge or permission was never spoken of directly, but "where ever it leads" was as close to a direct request for the unattainable as Cole ever got. The world of the hacker was as mysterious and wonderful to Cole as the domain of the surgeon. This was probably a result of his total inability to navigate the installation of the simplest piece of software.

The debt Randy owed Cole for getting him out of the small town paper in Southern California where Cole found him, and into the big league detective work of the *Chronicle* was paid long ago. The bond that remained gave the partnership of Sage & Callen an "us against the world" kind of Batman and Robin camaraderie that they both appreciated but never exploited.

"What are you looking for? I mean, in particular?" Randy probed.

"Don't know. I want to be fair in what I report, but I don't want to unnecessarily add to the myth and mystique of who he was." Cole's thoughts seemed to tumble out unintentionally. "What do you know about him?"

"I was at lunch one day and a homeless guy panhandling in front of Burger King told me that Jesse Monday could heal my hand. The old guy was convinced if I would go see 'Brother Jesse' that he would fix it good as new. I told the guy that it *was* good as new because I was born this way. He didn't think that was funny." Randy chuckled.

Randy Callen was born with a hand that was misshapen and looked more like a baby's foot than a hand. Although his hundred-watt personality covered for the layers of calluses built up from years of stares and comments, Cole knew that it was a source of embarrassment and was rarely spoken of.

"Did you go?" Cole asked.

"Yeah, right."

"Had to ask," Cole said.

"I did see him once by accident. He was out on The Avenues and a big crowd was following him. He crossed the street right in front of my car. He looked at me and smiled. Still gives me the shudders."

"Why's that?" Cole pressed.

"I don't know, something in his eyes, real, I don't know, otherworldly. How 'bout you? You ever see him?"

"Oh yeah, several times. I never was quite sure what to make of him."

"So you're not one of those 'God's other son' people?" Randy asked.

"No, not one of those," Cole said flatly, somewhat taken aback by Randy's question.

"Good, too many Kool-Aid drinkers in this city already. I'll get back with what I find."

"Thank you, sir." Cole hung up the phone.

"Here you go." Hanna handed Cole his mail across the desk.

On top of the stack was a small manila envelope. "Mr. Cole Sage" was handwritten across the front. The return address made no sense, though. In the upper left corner was a star, a snake, and what appeared to be a fingerprint, a thumbprint, really. The thing that didn't set right was the color of the print. It was a deep cordovan red.

"Where'd this come from?"

"It was left at reception. Shoot! I forgot the note." Hanna whirled around and returned to her desk. "This was in the other envelope. Sorry."

Random correspondences were nothing new. Cole filled his wastebasket with them a couple of times a week. Clippings, inner-office memos, assignments, story ideas, but usually they followed a more conventional to-and-from format.

The envelope wasn't sealed; the flap was just tucked in. Inside was a single yellow sheet from a legal pad, folded in thirds.

Dear Cole

I bet you never expected to hear from me again. I was your driver in 'Nam. You remember when I told you I wanted to be a writer. That dream was destroyed by the war. You are living my dream. So, I will give you a chance to write my story. We will win the war this time.

I'll be waiting.

Cole stared down at the abbreviation at the bottom corner, 10th PCH. No signature, no date, not even a clue as to what it was about. Yet, he couldn't just toss it in the trash.

Without even thinking, Cole tapped in the numbers of Randy Callen's line. Five rings, he was about to hang up and try later, when the panting voice of Cole's go-to researcher came on the line.

"Training for the Iron Man again?" Cole asked jovially.

"If you must know, I have started a juice fast and I have to pee every ten minutes."

"Can you tell me what 10th PCH is?"

"You ever heard of Google? You type things in and, magically, information pops up! An amazing invention." Randy chided.

"What kind of juice are you drinking? Snarkberry?"

"10th Public Affairs Detachment or Press Camp Headquarters," Randy offered, ignoring Cole's question. "Thinking of joining up?"

"Too late for that. Think you could get me a list of people attached to that office in Vietnam, 1972?"

"I'll see what I can do. Say, I have an extra bottle of kale, celery, beet, ginger, and carrot juice if you want to join me for lunch."

"Let me get back to you on that." Cole hung up to the sound of Randy's laughter.

Cole punched in the four digits for reception. "Hi, Cole Sage here, I got an envelope earlier. Did you see who delivered it?"

"He was just one of a dozen 'drop-offs' this morning."

"You don't recall who it was or what they looked like?" Cole pressed.

"Sorry, it was just a guy. He walks in, comes up and lays the envelope on the counter and walks out. Nothing about him sticks out in my memory. Security can review the camera feed from behind me," the receptionist offered.

"Thanks, it's not that big a deal." Cole hung up the phone.

"I don't have time for this," Cole grumbled, wadding up the note and tossing it and the envelope into the trash. With newborn determination, he spun around to his computer and went back to work on Jesse Monday's obituary.

THREE

A round two o'clock Cole hit a wall. Randy Callen was plunged headlong into the well of cyberspace data and wouldn't resurface for hours, the FedEx package from Carter Washington wouldn't arrive until morning and his last three calls were answered by voice mail. By three o'clock Cole was ready to escape. Various members of the staff came by his office with everything from requests for donations for a "Jesse's Lambs" orphanage, to elaborate conspiracy theories involving the NSA and Pat Robertson. It was time to go.

Pulling back into mid-afternoon traffic, Cole decided to go straight away and meet back with Jenny and Kelly. He always enjoyed sitting on the top deck of the floating house Kelly lived in on the Sausalito side of the Bay. By the time he finally passed the car fire on Geary and then sat for ten minutes trying to pull onto Van Ness, Cole decided it was a lost cause and headed for home.

The air was crisp and the sky was the kind they write greeting cards about to cheer people up. There was no way he would be stuck inside. When he finally pulled into the drive shortly after three-thirty, he decided to grab his bike and ride to Kelly's. He quickly changed into jeans and a sweatshirt and filled a water bottle.

Turning his blue Intel cap around so the wind wouldn't catch the bill and blow it into traffic, he headed toward the bridge. As he climbed and twisted his way up to the back entrance to the Golden Gate Bridge bikeway, Cole couldn't help but smile. The sight of windsurfers at the base of Fort Mason always made his heart feel light. As he watched the sailboards bounce and chop their way across the water, sails filling and gliding over the white caps, Cole seemed to feel lighter and faster as he pedaled harder and harder up the winding road to the bridge.

Clear days always brought people out in droves to walk, jog, and ride across the Golden Gate. Determined not to knock anyone down, Cole slowed and at times even walked his bike. It didn't matter because he loved just being on the bridge. At the halfway point he stopped and gazed back at the city. The crisp, clean air stung his cheeks. Far below, a freighter, decks stacked with cargo containers, passed into the bay. A young German couple Cole took for honeymooners, stopped and laughed, and hugged near him, as they pointed at the landmarks on the skyline.

"Alcatraz, Alcatraz!" The rosy-cheeked woman squealed and pointed excitedly, her pale blue eyes dancing as she made the connection between her airport tourist map and the Rock in the middle of the bay.

Cole wanted to comment or just be part of their excitement but realized his four or five words of

German would probably not make for any kind of meaningful dialog. He smiled at the couple and rode on.

When he arrived at the dock where Kelly's house was moored, Jenny was down for a nap. Kelly was heating some leftover chicken noodle soup for a snack and Cole helped by digging around the cupboards until he found a box of saltine crackers.

"Up top?" Kelly said, setting two steaming mugs onto a tray.

"Read my mind!" Cole said pointing toward the door with the box of crackers.

On the top deck, Cole pulled two chairs around to the lee side of the divider wall that acted as a windbreak. They settled into the chairs and each took a mug.

"Nothing in the world better than chicken noodle soup with lots of crackers." Cole smiled and crushed a half-full plastic tube of crackers.

"You mean nothing better than a little soup with your crackers." Kelly frowned at his desecration of her homemade offering.

"You don't like crackers?"

"I like you," she said coyly.

"Funny girl," Cole said pushing crackers into the soup with the backside of his spoon.

They ate in silence for several minutes. The banners on the lines of the floating house next door snapped and popped in the wind. Cole was so used to eating soup from a red and white can that it took him a minute to realize that Kelly made the soup from scratch, noodles and all.

"I love these noodles," he offered.

"Nice save," Kelly said, giving him a forgiving smile. "Cole," she was obviously choosing her words. "What are you going to write about Jesse Monday?"

There it is, Cole thought. "How do you mean?" He always answered a question with a question when he needed time to gather his thoughts.

"Hero, villain, con-man, righteous servant, God's messenger, Satan's tool, divider, healer, how will you portray him?"

"Truthfully," Cole answered, watching for her response.

"And that is?"

"What I will try to find out in the next few days." Cole took a big spoonful of soup and admired the ratio of cracker to fluid. "You know, if you do it right, you can put in just enough cracker to absorb the fluid and make the crackers soft and moist without ending up with a dry bowl of dust."

"You're avoiding the question. What do you think of him?"

"*Did* I think of him?" Cole said, correcting the tense of Kelly's question.

"What is the point of killing someone like him? I mean there is a crackpot on every corner, right? Half the channels on TV have somebody espousing some goofy philosophy." Kelly stared into the mug as she stirred her soup. "Seems so pointless."

"All murder is pointless."

"But some are understandable. Like gangsters and drug dealers, they kill each other all the time. It's not right, but it is part of their world. If you live by the sword, you know, but to kill a preacher?"

"They killed *The Preacher* too."

"Well, Monday certainly wasn't Him."

"Lot of folks seemed to think he was. I think one of them was Chris Ramos."

"You're kidding."

"Chuck has asked me to look into this whole mess and find..." Cole made two quotation marks with his fingers in the air. "The truth. Turns out that Chris was one of Jesse Monday's fans."

"I don't know if fan is the right word for this," Kelly said.

"Probably not. The problem is that this assignment is not business, it's personal, at least for Chuck. He needs answers on a spiritual level. He wants me to find a 'truth' that will assure him he will see Chris in heaven."

"He said that?"

"Not in so many words, but his meaning was pretty clear." Cole shrugged.

"So where do you start?" The process Cole used to research a story always fascinated Kelly.

"This time I've called in the cavalry. I called my contact at the FBI and I have Randy Callen doing his snoop thing. I should have something by morning to get me started."

"Then we can have a nice evening and not have to worry about where you start. I say we go out for burgers when Jenny wakes up and eat by the pier. She loves to watch the gulls."

"I'm thinking bacon, grilled onions, and extra cheese." Cole grinned.

"I'm thinking veggie burger, extra lettuce for you, Mr. 170 over 80 blood pressure."

"I rode my bike here," Cole pleaded. "Grilled onions and regular cheese?"

"That will be OK, I guess." Kelly smiled, then added, "On a veggie burger."

* * *

Cole kissed Jenny on the top of the head, and she enthusiastically waved good-bye as he pedaled up the dock. Kelly called Erin to let her know that she was on her way with Jenny. Cole arrived home just as the last light of dusk was slipping away. He kicked off his shoes in the entryway and headed for the kitchen. The red light on the answering machine flashed in the half-light. Cole hit the play button.

"You have two messages," the robotic voice reported.

"Hey, it's Randy. Pick up. Are you there? Got a bunch of stuff for you. Are you gonna pick up? No? See you in the morning then." The robotic voice reported that the message from Randy Callen came in a 4:38 p.m.

A broad smile crossed Cole's face as the second message bubbled from the machine, "Hi grandpa! Did you get home O.K.? I hope you're not too tired from too much fun. Love you." There was a pause, then Cole could hear Erin in the background saying something he couldn't make out. "And mom says no ice cream!" Again the sound was muffled. "Be a good boy and keep on your diet. What? We want you here for a long time! Bye!" Jenny's laugh was the last thing he heard as she hung up. The machine reported her call came in about five minutes before he got home.

Cole held it to one scoop of ice cream while he channel-surfed. For once he went to bed early.

Early to bed, Cole thought as he plopped the morning paper on the kitchen table. The front page seemed to explode with the news of Jesse Monday's shooting. A picture of Monday with his arms spread, head back, being carried by some of his followers to an ambulance covered nearly the entire page above the fold. The headline screamed "Death of a Miracle Man" just below the banner.

The paramedic stood at the open ambulance door. His expression was what grabbed Cole. It was as if he had no control of the situation and was powerless to do his job. His hands were half-raised in a questioning gesture and deep furrows creased his brow.

Monday's eyes were closed and his mouth was gaping open. A big man was holding his feet at the ankles. Two other men supported most of his weight, their hands under his shoulders and back. At first glance, Cole thought, *you would think he was on a cross.*

The details of the article were sketchy at best. The time and place were as concrete as it got. The shooter was described only as a person dressed in a black sweatshirt with the hood up. No one seemed to see where the shooter came from or went. Monday's wounds were not specifically identified, only that he was hit in the "chest area." He was taken to St. Mary's Medical Center on Stanyan Street because the shooting occurred outside a Starbuck's on Fulton. He died on the five-block ride to the hospital.

The body was later transported to the Bryant Mortuary on Fulton. Somehow, it never arrived. There was no explanation of how the body disappeared during the transport of a mere sixteen blocks. The morgue technician, a Topher Saldono, claims he turned over the body at the back door to a couple of guys in dark suits from the funeral home at 11:15 pm. The funeral director says no such pick-up was ever made.

When Cole arrived at *The Chronicle*, the first thing he noticed was the number of black armbands being worn by the staff. Others wore lapel pins with messages like "Remember Jesse," "Expect a Miracle" or "He Will Be Back". As he passed through the main office he was struck by how many desks and cubicles bore some form of tribute to Jesse Monday, everywhere, flowers and pictures with each individual's personal message. "Jesse Mended My Broken Heart and his Killer Has Broken it Again." was pinned to the outside wall of the cubicle of a woman who sat at her desk, her face resting in her hands.

The mood and stunned silence in the building reminded Cole of a long-ago November day. He could almost feel the heavy sensation of shock mixed with grief hovering in the room. The gray clouds outside his classroom windows seemed to add to the despair. Cole was in the sixth grade. Just four days after his birthday and just a few days until Thanksgiving, it was just like any other day, until the secretary came and handed his teacher a slip of paper. Cole never forgot the look that crossed Mrs. Van Camp's face. A teacher was someone from a different world in those days; they had no first names and represented a power and authority that has long been replaced by privacy laws and students' rights. On this day, though, Joan Van Camp became another heartbroken American, like those who cried and choked on the words that told us that our President was assassinated in Dallas. That day everyone was sent home early. Eighth graders wept openly and everyone stood around as if somehow the world had come to an end.

As he walked to his office, Cole felt a strange disconnect from those around him. He did not share their sense of shock and heartbreak. He was saddened by the death of a person he knew, but he never bought into the Jesse Monday, "second coming," "new messiah," "God's anointed one," "Jesus for a new age" hysteria.

"Good morning," Hanna said, smiling up at Cole.

"So, what do you think of all this?" Cole said, giving a sweeping motion across the wide ocean of cubicles.

"I'm Jewish. We've had a million wanna-be prophets, including, your Yeshua. I think they had the right idea when they used to stone them," Hanna said, enjoying her own remark.

"Alrighty then.

Cole pulled the door of his office half-closed and sat down. On top of his desk was a file folder at least two inches thick with a rubber band around it. Randy Callen didn't waste any time compiling data on Jesse Monday. As he began thumbing through the material inside, Cole grabbed a yellow note pad and started scribbling phrases, names, and notes of his own. Lost in the research, and formulating the direction of the piece he would write, he didn't notice Hanna's knock on his doorframe until she rapped harder and cleared her throat.

"FedEx for you," Hanna said as she approached the desk. "Requires your signature, too."

Cole scribbled his name across the line after the X, "Thank you."

"You're welcome," came from a different voice in the room.

"Randy! Hey, you must have burned the midnight oil." Cole indicated he take a seat.

"Here is a bit more, but I thought I would hand-deliver it."

"Why's that?"

"You might call it "sensitive" material," Randy said, passing a manila envelope to Cole.

"There's more to all this than meets the eye, isn't there." Cole smiled.

"What the hell's going on around this place anyway? Has everybody been 'podded'?"

Cole laughed in appreciation of his young friend's *Invasion of the Body Snatchers* reference. "Sure feels like it. I had no idea so many people were impacted by Monday. It might be a good idea just for self-preservation if we kept our skepticism to ourselves. This love of Jesse goes all the way to the top and could be a real wedge issue. No sense creating ill will that might reap unwanted future problems."

"Got it. You seem deep into it. I'll get back to work. If you need any more 'background' let me know." Randy stood to go.

Cole picked up the Fed Ex envelope and waved it over his desk. "With what you found, and a little help from a friend in Washington, I think I'll have enough to get me going. Thanks for getting to this so fast."

"Ours is to serve and obey." Randy gave Cole a very unmilitary salute and was gone.

"Well, Jesse, what's your story?" Cole said aloud, tearing open the package from Carter Washington.

Most of the biographical information on Jesse Monday was well documented and part of his public presentation. Jesse's mother Marcia was an unwed mother-to-be, of seventeen, when her parents shipped her off to live with an older cousin in Sacramento. The cousin was another black sheep who didn't fall in line with the strict tenets of the extremely rigid offshoot sect of the Pentecostal Holiness Church.

Marcia and her cousin Billie hit it off immediately. They both broke with the strict teachings of their denomination. The Elders, who would have led the congregation to believe they were wanton women, were far from the truth of who they actually were.

Billie worked a part-time job at a fabric shop. She also had a fiancé, Zack, who worked in the building trades and helped with the groceries. Marcia cleaned, cooked, mended and washed Zack's clothes. Since Zack supplied most of the food he was a welcome addition to their dinner table.

There were strict rules of the house and Zack was banished after ten o'clock. This seemed strange to their circle of friends since one of the girls was already pregnant. There was a moral code and a strong sense of propriety the girls lived by. They still attended a small church near their apartment and neither smoked, drank or used drugs.

One evening Zack brought his friend from work, Joel Monday, to the apartment for dinner. Joel was a tall redhead, ten years older than Marcia, with skin sunbaked and rough as dried leaves. He was smitten with Marcia from the start.

Marcia explained to Joel that the father of her unborn child was a traveling gospel singer who did a concert at her church. Her parents brought him home for dinner and offered him a room to help save on his expenses. All through dinner he paid close attention to Marcia and once slipped his hand onto her thigh. That night when the house was quiet he slipped into her room and had taken her. She knew nothing of men and was flattered by his kisses, but was ashamed and confused by what he did to her. When her belly began to swell, she understood better, but her parents called her "Eve the beguiler" and sent her away.

Marcia and Joel were married six weeks after they met. Joel took his new bride to a small town ninety miles south of Sacramento called Keyes, where they would live out the rest of their lives together.

Jesse Joel Monday was born shortly after midnight on September 29, 1985. He was by all accounts a happy, well-adjusted little boy who loved to follow his dad around and mimicked his use of a measuring tape, saw, and hammer. JJ, as he was nicknamed, loved to go to Sunday School at the little church his parents attended. Although he was a bright boy, he tended to daydream and was never considered a great student. Jesse frequently received poor marks because he seemed to be able to turn any assignment into a religious argument.

Shortly after his twelfth birthday, during a children's Christmas pageant, Jesse put aside the prepared text he was supposed to read and gave a fifteen-minute sermon. Marcia and Joel sat in stunned disbelief as the congregation called out support and encouragement to the freckled kid at the pulpit.

From time to time, Jesse was called upon to speak at youth meetings and on several occasions stepped into the pulpit when the pastor was sick or on vacations. On all occasions, the response was one of surprise and respect for the wisdom shown by one so young. Jesse finished school and followed Joel into the family business. Monday Construction did well and was highly respected as house framers. With all their success, though, Jesse was restless and often spoke of a higher calling.

He began to give "spiritual talks" during lunch breaks. More and more frequently the men would be late getting back to work because they were more than willing to listen to Jesse's stories. Joel found it increasingly difficult to excuse Jesse's crew for not meeting deadlines. Although never confrontational, always repentant and begging forgiveness, Jesse knew that he could not continue the life of a construction worker when he felt such a strong calling to preach.

Somehow Joel always knew there would never be a Monday & Sons Construction. When Jesse decided to strike out on his own and try the life of a traveling preacher, Joel wasn't all that surprised. Truth be told, he was surprised it took as long as it did.

With the help of his pastor, Jesse was able to get a few speaking engagements around California and Nevada. Soon the pulpits of small churches and "preaching to the choir" lost their appeal. Along with a rough-and-tumble Arkansas transplant, Skeeter Evans, an ex-con farmhand from the neighboring town of Hughson, who was part carnival barker and part security guard, Jesse began to hold the first of his outside meetings. Usually, they happened at parks or bus stations where homeless people gathered of an evening.

Standing on a bench or picnic table, Skeeter would begin calling out to the people in the area to gather around and listen to what his friend was about to say. Whether they gathered or not, Jesse would begin walking around and in a loud, clear voice, begin telling a story that, in the end, was a fable designed to teach a spiritual lesson. His "wandering" style never failed to attract a crowd. Before long, the "storytelling preacher" was attracting big enough crowds that the police would regularly show up and try to disperse the crowd.

Since his message was a positive one, the police usually caught on and let the impromptu meeting continue. It was during a roll-up by the police that Gary Timmons first heard Jesse speak. The next week he left the Stockton Police Department and began to travel with Jesse.

In the early spring, word spread of a large anti-war protest that was planned at the gates of the Lawrence Livermore Laboratories, a large weapons development facility nestled in the coastal range not far from San Francisco. Jesse, Skeeter, and Gary arrived just as the protesters started arriving and Jesse began to speak to them.

"There once was a farmer with a small flock of sheep. The sheep were his pride and joy. In fact, the farmer was so fond of the sheep he gave them all names. His children played with the sheep and the farmer's wife used their wool to make socks and sweaters for their family. The sheep were never killed for food.

"One night a pack of wolves came and killed one of the sheep. When the farmer found 'Belle' lying dead the next morning, he was grieved as if it was one of his children. The whole family stood around a grave the farmer dug under a big oak tree to show their respect for the lost sheep.

"A few nights later the wolves got 'Sam the Ram.' Again the family wept and buried their friend, the sheep. The wolves were running wild across the countryside killing sheep and chickens, ducks, turkeys, and even dogs.

"The farmer's wife asked why nothing was done to stop them.

"What can be done?" the farmer replied.

"I would think the wolves must be killed to stop the slaughter of our animals," she answered.

"But I have nothing to kill them with, except a shovel or hoe."

"Then that will have to do," the wife replied.

The next night the farmer waited, and sure enough, as the moon rose to light the night sky, the pack of wolves attacked the flock. The farmer took his hoe and ran against the wolves. He hit several with the hoe but they turned on him and savagely attacked him.

In the morning the farmer's wife found him on the porch of their farmhouse. He bled to death from the wounds he received from the wolves tearing his flesh."

"What's the point?" yelled a grey-haired woman with a sign reading 'Make Peace with All Men.'"

"The point is, countries must defend them-selves and just as 'Saul slayed his thousands, and David his ten thousands,' in days of old, we have enemies that would destroy us. Shall we let them attack us with bigger and better weapons? Will we attack with just a shovel or hoe? I tell you this, it is far more important to assure your place in heaven than to worry about the 'what if's' of the next war. There has always been, and always will be, wars. It just seems a waste of energy, protesting something you cannot stop.

"We should be more concerned with the hearts and souls of our enemies than what the government is doing, which we have no power over. We should grieve for our enemies kind of like the farmer's sheep. If we really love them, we should be concerned with where they'll be if we should find them dead in the morning. Perhaps we should all go out and share our love across the ocean. It would probably bear much more fruit than this protest, don't you think?" Jesse smiled at the woman with the sign.

"Sounds good, but..."

"There are no buts that can't be overcome if we really love our fellow man." Jesse turned his palms up in a gesture that asked, "So, what are you going to do?"

"I'm no religious fanatic," a man in the crowd yelled out.

"That's fine. Start with just being a fanatic. Seems you got that down." Many in the crowd laughed. "Now try turning it on the wolves. Who knows, your faith may grow from the love you share. Listen, if we really love our fellow man and are truly against war, let us start with changing hearts. We could all probably use a change of heart of our own, couldn't we? Then let's work on our enemies so they will become our friends."

As Jesse turned to walk to another large group of people, he was approached by four young men wearing cowboy hats and dusty boots.

"What kind of preacher are you?" the youngest-looking of the four asked.

"Best I can be," Jesse replied.

"I never heard anybody put things the way you did. Kind of made sense to me."

"We're the Fischer brothers. We've been talking, and we would like to join up."

"Join up?"

"Yeah. We believe in what you said and all and think we should do something to spread the word."

"We got a truck, too. We could haul stuff for you," another brother offered.

"Well, this is all the stuff I have." Jesse held out a backpack. "But I think you four would be a great asset to our merry band."

* * *

Cole flipped over several pictures and read the caption attached to the back. The black-and-white surveillance shots showed Jesse preaching to the crowds, climbing into the back of a pick-up, and with his hand on top of the head of a homeless man with matted hair and a scraggly beard. The captions identified the date, place and several people in the shot.

A sheet of paper clipped to the last photo stamped "CLASSIFIED" caught Cole's eye. The document contained an FBI field agent's report on "curious activities" going on at one of Jesse's meetings. Several faces were circled in red felt-tip pen. All were dark, heavily bearded and looked Middle Eastern.

The paragraph read:

Several members of a radical Muslim cell known as The New Al-Nusra Brigade, were in attendance at a rally held 3/13/14 on the campus of UC Santa Cruz. The speaker, Jesse Monday, made no direct contact with members of the Brigade, however, two of his entourage met with Brigade members after the rally. One of the men, known as Skeeter Evans, has been linked to various anti-government, white supremacist militias in the Southern United States. The other man is unknown to the Bureau.

Cole closed the folder and leaned back in his chair. On the occasions he was near Jesse Monday or attended one of his meetings, there was never an overtly anti-government message. It was always the same frothy, peace-love-truth message draped in Jesse's "aw-shucks" parables.

Skeeter always seemed to Cole as not quite in step with the message. Bristly, unsmiling, and almost hostile most of the time, there was little if any manifestation of Jesse's "Truth" in him.

Cole pulled the picture out of the folder again. Three faces in red circles, and not more than ten feet away, looking in their direction was Skeeter. The idea of Muslim terrorists joining forces with red-neck radicals seemed silly at first. As Cole pondered the possible benefits for each, he kept returning to one common goal, bring down the government of the United States.

Jesse Monday morphed into something far afield from the freckle-faced boy in the little Pentecostal church where he grew up. Could he have been behind the anarchist leanings of his right-hand man? He strayed from Christian doctrine but could he swallow the Seven Pillars of Islam? What was this truth he so generously spoke of and offered up to his followers, yet never defined? It seemed a far stretch for Cole that this man of peace, and teacher of a better way, could be building an army of followers hell-bent on overthrowing the government.

Then it struck him. Maybe it was everyone's plan but his. What if Jesse was just a means to an end for Skeeter and his band of "don't worry, we'll take care of it" handlers. Cole sat up straight in his chair and spread the contents of Carter Washington's files across his desk.

"This could *really* be a story." Cole scanned the documents in front of him.

Draped in the metaphorical robes of Jesse as a holy man, forces of an entirely different kind of belief system had been using Jesse Monday. The voice of peace and "truth" was simply the means of drawing a crowd; the other message would come later.

Cole rubbed his forehead. Did Jesse know about it, was he in on the ploy? Or did he get wise to what was being planned in his name and object?

"Come on, Sage," Cole ran his fingers over the material in front of him. "You're way out on a limb here."

Participant or pawn, one thing was certain about Jesse Monday. Either way, he was dead.

FOUR

From his early days as a cub reporter on his high school newspaper, Cole kept a small spiral notepad in his pocket. It was now as much a part of his daily dress as putting on shoes or double-checking that his wallet was in his pocket. The evolution of his "memory checker" progressed from the ten-cent original to his deeply scarred, yet ever-faithful, leather-covered version that Ellie bought him as a birthday present in college.

To anyone else, Cole's filing system would appear to be a disheveled mess of file folders, report folders, and little spiral note pads, but to Cole, it was moments away from providing him with instant memory and recall. In the great scheme of things, going back three years to track Cole's coverage of Jesse Monday was a simple task. As he flipped through the note pads he stopped to read his notes on other stories he'd covered. The mayoral race, a Noe Valley arson fire, the reopening of the DeYoung Museum, quotes from the governor, the President of Chile's visit to San Francisco, three or four movie star interviews about global warming, the ramblings of a couple of aging rock stars, and a "religious rally in the park."

The strange thing about Cole's notes was the way they seemed to transport him back to a place or time where he could almost relive the moment. Jesse Monday and his band of religious street people were nothing new by the time of the "Great Golden Gate Rally," as it came to be known, and his notebook offered a familiarity that took Cole back to one of the strangest events he ever covered.

By all estimates, nearly five thousand people showed up to hear Jesse "give the truth" in Golden Gate Park. The forecast was for rain, and the clouds that rolled in from the Pacific were so black, it seemed like they would drop from the sky with the weight of the moisture they carried. At ten o'clock Cole decided he would stay in his office and do some research on a piece he was working on. News of the planned purchase of nearly a block of North Beach apartments and businesses raised the ire of everyone from the Mayor to the North Beach Merchants Association.

Paradigm Engineering, a firm known for the demolition of old San Francisco neighborhoods, and the creation of newer "soulless" modern structures, proposed a new round of their "into the future" projects. Cole was given the file and asked to do a multipart article on preserving San Francisco's neighborhoods and architectural heritage. Around eleven-fifteen, he headed for the restroom and caught a glimpse out the window. The sun was shining and there wasn't a cloud in sight. He could still make it to the rally. Why not? Cole thought. There's no fear of coming back soaked.

The atmosphere was more like the buzz before a concert in the park by an over-the-hill rocker, trying to bring back the Summer of Love, than an outdoor church service. Cole parked behind Kezar Stadium and walked to Speedway Meadow. The meadow and side of the hill were covered with a patchwork of blankets and people. A huge banner that proclaimed, "The Truth Is Free" formed a kind of gateway to the meadow. The crowd hummed with excitement as Cole made his way to the edge of the crowd, as close to the front as he felt he dared press.

Jesse Monday took the makeshift stage within minutes of Cole being seated. There was no warm-up, no introduction. One moment the stage was bare, the next Jesse stood, hands in his back pockets, looking out over the crowd.

"A lot of you came here today because some-body told you, 'This guy's got some good things to say.'" Jesse began. His voice was strong and seemed to roll across the meadow like San Francisco fog. "Some of you heard that a blind man was healed and threw away his white cane and gave his Seeing Eye dog back. But I am here to tell you that many of you are as blind as he was."

The silence that fell over the crowd was broken by a wave of murmuring that seemed to move from back to front.

"This isn't about nice words and clever stories. Chico the blind man healed himself. Power comes from faith, faith comes from Truth and I am here to show you the way to Truth. Are you sick? You want to get well, be healed, get better, whatever you want to

call it, it's yours right now. Trouble is, you don't believe. The Truth is in each of us.

"I am here to tell you that if you have reached
the end of the line if you are hanging on by the last
thread in that rope if you are without hope, you are
the lucky ones. All you need to do is look up to
heaven; it's yours for the taking. You realize that
Truth is your only way out. When your spirit is bank-
rupt, heaven is your reward.

"I want you to look around this beautiful park,
look around at all these people here. Death walks
among us. I don't mean like in some ghost story, no
spooky heebie-jeebies foolishness. I'm talking about
the pain and sorrow that grief has etched across many
of the faces I see today. Loss is a pain that comes to
all; how we deal with it is a gift of God. Listen to me,
turn your eyes inside and you'll feel His big arms
around you. Take heart because day by day you find
comfort in knowing the Truth is with you.

"Now, I got a word or two for those of you sitting in the back, shakin' in your boots and afraid to
speak to the person on your left or your right. Those
of you who slipped in with the crowd and let the
pushy ones get past you; getting all the seats up front,
listen to me! You guys are the ones this is for. You're
going to be the ones who will carry on for me. You're
the ones who will bring what this world needs, wants
really, and you guys are the ones who are like aloe on a
sunburn, a soothing presence in a world gone crazy.
I'm telling you, this world is yours because you will be

the last ones standing when the rest of the crazies have jumped off the cliff."

To the right of where Jesse stood came a gut-wrenching scream, like a primal animal howl; the deep fluid tearing of vocal cords sent a cold wave of fear through the crowd. Cole turned just as a man with dreadlocks and a matted beard leaped into the crowd. Filthy, mud-covered and completely naked, the man began to dance and twirl and scream, head back, jerking and twitching spasmodically. His eyes were rolled back in his head and the whites possessed a yellow jaundiced cast.

"Touch God, touch me!" the man screamed. "What are you, Jesse Monday? Are you God's chosen one? The Messiah? A prince of the Kingdom of God? Are you God's Son?" The man threw himself on the ground and began rolling and kicking at those around him. People scurried and jumped up from their blankets. Mothers grabbed their children and held them close to their breasts. Several men tried to grab the man but he fought loose and spit and screamed at them.

Without notice, Jesse made his way into the crowd and stood no more than ten feet from where the crazed man spun, arms outstretched, and howling like the very soul of madness. As he moved into the crowd, Cole slipped a few feet behind Jesse and followed him to see just what he would do.

"You need to be still," Jesse said softly.

The man instantly stopped spinning around and faced Jesse. "What have you to do with me?"

"You are possessed by an evil you have no defense against."

In a completely different voice than before, the man screamed. "We know who you are!"

"You have said enough." Jesse stretched his hand out toward the man. With eyes closed, he began to say something so softly Cole could not hear.

Moments before, the man was an energy force of noise, sinew, and fierce violent movement. He now stood perfectly still, his hands folded and covering his groin. "We do not fear you, Jesse Monday," he growled.

"Release this man and be gone." The voice that came from Jesse was deeper and projected far beyond where the man stood.

A large flock of seagulls, hopping and fluttering just beyond the edge of the crowd near the trash cans along the tree line, began to squawk and scream. Several attacked each other. Then, as with one set of wings, the flock took off and soared high into the afternoon sun.

The man once full of rage and uncontrollable movement fell limp upon the grass.

"What is your name?" Jesse said, kneeling next to where the man lay motionless.

"David," the man said in a calm voice.

"Someone get our brother David a blanket," Jesse spoke to a group standing just beyond the man. "David, I want you to go home. Get cleaned up. Your family misses you."

A woman in the crowd draped a quilt over David's shoulders. With gentle, non-threatening movements David crawled toward Jesse. As he reached where the preacher stood, David lay face down and began kissing Jesse's feet.

"No need for that. Get up and do what I asked. Go home."

David stood and looked Jesse in the face for a long moment, then, without a word, slowly walked through the crowd and across the grass to the trees and disappeared. Jesse walked back to the stage, and as if nothing happened, he began to speak right where he left off.

"There are those of you who came here with the purest of motives. You long to be clean, to live clean and long, to do what is right. I want you to understand clearly you will get what you want. Your hearts and minds know your desire is real. Like food and water, you're sure you cannot survive without knowing truth. You don't have to worry about what is to come because you're already on the right path. Can you feel it? Your needs and the deepest longings of your heart are being met.

"You have heard it said, 'Judge not lest you be judged'. I want you to take it a step further. Let me tell you a story." Jesse smiled as the crowd gave a knowing laugh of approval. "A long time ago a wife came to the king after hearing her husband had been arrested." He paused again. "Now these guys had no three-strikes law. With them it was one strike, you're dead.

"Please, oh great king, let my man go!" the woman pleaded.

"Why should I?" asked the king. "He has been caught twice stealing chickens. Justice must be served, he must die!"

"'I am not asking for justice,' the wife cried. 'I plead for mercy!'

"'Your husband doesn't deserve mercy!' the king yelled.

"'Your Highness,' the woman said. 'It wouldn't be mercy if he deserved it!'

"'Then I will show mercy because there is no one who deserves it less.' And the king saved the woman's husband from the gallows." Jesse smiled at the crowd.

"Remember this, that old king was far richer because of his mercy to the undeserving thief, and the same will happen when you show undeserved kindness.

"You are people of good hearts and many have marched, and spoken out for peace for many years. I want everyone who hears my voice to remember this simple truth. It is you who are truly the children of God! We as a people have shed too much blood in the name of religion and God. I tell you this; it is not the warrior who spreads the word of God's love, but the lovers of peace."

Many in the meadow jumped up and applauded.

As they settled back and quieted down again, Jesse raised his hand and spoke louder and clearer than before. "A lot of you have been made fun of because you came out here today. A lot more of you will be teased, poked fun at, and I'm afraid some will suffer worse. Some may even be beaten up and maybe worse for coming down on the side of what you know to be true. We are about the Truth, and the Truth will truly set you free. But know this, friends; you will be the ones looking down from heaven into the very pit of hell on those who have persecuted you for your faith! Walk in the Truth!"

The crowd seemed to all jump to their feet at once. The cheers and applause were deafening. As Cole looked around, many mixed their laughter and applause with tears streaming down their faces. People young and old embraced, shook hands, patted each other on the back and seemed to bask in the joy of having been together. Around the crowd, though, were those who spoke without smiles. Some covered their mouths and they spoke to those next to them. Many in the crowd began to leave. Small groups around the meadow joined hands to sing and pray. Lines formed, then blurred, and then disappeared altogether as the crowds pressed in to get a chance to speak to Jesse.

A group of men Cole pegged for handlers, followers, or maybe hangers-on were gathered around Jesse, controlling and directing the flow of people and the make-up of those reaching him. Every so often, someone would be hustled off to the side and "encouraged" to leave.

The tallest of the men stood with his arms folded at the corner of the stage overlooking the meadow and keeping a close eye on the throng of people pressing ever forward to catch a closer look or a word with Jesse. Cole hopped up on the stage and extended a hand to the man.

"Hello, I'm Cole Sage with the *San Francisco Chronicle*," Cole said to the man glaring at him, arms still folded. "Okay, we'll try this a different way. What's your name?"

"Skeeter Evans and Jesse don't do interviews."

"That will save me a lot of asking him questions then. How about you? Will he let you talk?"

"Let me?" Skeeter laughed. "Nobody tells me what to do."

"So tell me then, what's your job with the group?"

"I like to think I'm the guy second in charge. I keep things from," Skeeter paused, trying to be sure he used the right words, "becoming unpleasant."

"For who?"

"Anybody, but mostly I keep the crackpots away from Jesse."

"There's been trouble in the past?" Cole asked.

For the first time, Skeeter smiled. "You got your run-of-the-mill crazies; wanna-be prophets and the like. Mostly, church leaders are the real problem. Preachers are a real pain, you know, always trying to prove Jesse wrong, accuse him of stuff."

"Accuse him? He sounds pretty straight forward to me."

"There is a lot of talk about some of the things he's done, so-called healings, stuff like that. Wouldn't you think that they would welcome someone like Jesse? But no, sir, they are always trying to pick a fight. Other day a priest came up and told Jesse he was going to hell. Imagine, Jesse, going to hell. He's the new Christ."

There it was. This was what was suggested, argued about, and was the center of the whole Jesse Monday controversy. Now Cole heard it from his number one man.

"Let me ask you something, Skeeter." Cole was going to tread lightly. "When you say the "new" Christ, do you mean like a replacement for Jesus, or Jesse is Jesus come back for a second go-round, or what?"

Skeeter unfolded his arms and turned to face Cole. His skin was tanned and heavily lined. The circles of sunglasses showed in the lighter skin around his eyes and seemed to deepen their blue. "So what's your angle? Cult Rises in the City by the Bay? Would-be Messiah Deceives Followers? Second Coming? Of what? You guys are all alike, trying to tear down the good Jesse tries to do."

"For being the right hand of such a positive guy, you're a real barrel of grump. What about all this 'Truth' stuff? Seems to me a little truth around here would help your cause. You can't even give a straight answer." Cole shook his head. "My angle? Trying to get a look at the real Jesse Monday. It would seem to me that you do such a good job keeping the press away that nobody knows who he is. Seems to me you would want an accurate portrait of the man who would save the world."

"And who is going to do this accurate portrait? You?"

"Yeah. So, how about this? If you don't let him do interviews, just let me hang out with you guys. Let me see what's going on from the inside. Unless you got something to hide." Cole waited. He knew the first one to speak was the loser in this negotiation.

"First off," Skeeter began.

Cole had him.

"Nobody speaks for Jesse but Jesse. I just try to keep things plumb. Second, there is nothing we hide from anybody."

"So you'll let me tag along for a while?"

Skeeter stood for a long moment, studying Cole. "We don't need publicity. People, that's what gets the word out. So don't play like you're doing us any favors. The most important thing you could do would be the first person in the media to tell the truth."

"What is the truth? As you see it, Skeeter?"

"The Truth is in all of us, Jesse shows the way to it. He is God's earthly manifestation. Jesse is the one mankind has been waiting for."

"Like Jesus?" Cole pressed.

"Jesus, Jesse, Jesse, Jesus—they are one and the same. God is one, you know? Jesse didn't ask for this anointing, it was his from birth. Okay, I give you there are a lot of parallels with the other Savior. This time it's different."

"How's that?" Cole needed to get closer to the core beliefs of this new "Savior."

"This time peace will come from Jesse's words. Wars will end, hatred, bigotry, racism, all those 'isms' will cease to be. And Truth will rule."

"Nice idea. Noble, lofty, goals." Cole paused. "Why Jesse, though? What makes him the one?"

"Prophecy. Jesse is prophecy fulfilled. Isaiah 11:10 says 'He will include and attract people from all cultures and nations.' You ever seen such a mixed bag in your life as this bunch here? You think this is an accident? Isaiah 52:7 says 'He will be a messenger of peace.' The Truth brings peace."

"Okay, but it seems to me you can apply that to any spiritual leader or rock star, even. I mean, you quote Isaiah but I seem to remember something about a virgin birth, the lineage of King David, being born in Bethlehem. Unless I got it all wrong, Jesse isn't even Jewish, which is a major prerequisite for being the Messiah."

"Jews!" Skeeter nearly spit the word out. "History was robbed of the true meaning of the ancient scriptures by the Papists who did the so-called translations. There were no Jews before 400 A.D.! All this 'God's chosen people'. In the original text it doesn't say 'chosen,' it says 'separate' or 'put aside.' They were the unwashed, unwanted Semite tribes, always trying to stir up trouble."

"So, Jesus was what, then?"

"Most of what you call the New Testament was a fairy story of a prophet that they so desperately needed that the so-called 'Jews' grabbed onto the stories and blew them all out of whack. All these stories of Jesus of Nazareth and of Muhammad and Buddha are only intended to pave the way for the Anointed King and to prepare the world to worship God together. You want a quote? How about this one: 'For then I shall turn a clear tongue to the nations to call all in the Name of the Lord and to worship him.' That clear tongue, that messenger of God's final truth, is Jesse Monday."

Cole smiled and tried not to let his thoughts show on his face. "So Jesse is God."

Skeeter shook his head. "Everything for the nonbeliever is so easy to put in a box."

"Take a mighty big box to put God in," Cole offered.

"What would you call one who has power over the demonic spirits, over disease and death, and even over the forces of nature?"

"That's a lot to claim. Are you saying that description fits Jesse?"

"You just saw him cast out demons and send them to that flock of gulls. His healings have been witnessed time and again."

"David, the mentally ill guy Jesse calmed down, was possessed? And when the gulls flew off so did the demons? That's a bit of stretch, but okay. Power over death, really?" Cole was not going to let this claim go unchallenged.

"The time will come. It's not time quite yet, but it will come."

The men controlling the crowd began to circulate. Cole could hear them telling the people waiting to see Jesse that they might as well go home, Jesse would be leaving shortly. A few turned and moved away from the crowd, a few used the opening to press closer.

"Tonight we're having dinner at the home of some friends. If you really are looking for the Truth, you're welcome to come. I am taking you at your word. No interview." Skeeter's words were more of a warning than a statement of fact.

"Agreed. I just want to see Jesse off the stage and with friends."

Skeeter wrote something on the back of a business card and handed it to Cole. "Here's the address. We eat at six, nothing fancy, but you're welcome to join us. God isn't mocked, you remember that.

* * *

The home of Miki and Mini Morgan was wedged between two empty flats on a very short side street off Pacheco. The twins were very petite, almost fragile in their build and demeanor, yet open, friendly and very welcoming. The house was clean, and though the furnishing seemed sparse, there was a feeling of a home well used. Above the desk in the entryway was a photograph of a severe-looking black man and an

Asian woman with long straight hair, who immediately made Cole think of the Mona Lisa.

"Our parents," a small voice said from behind Cole. "I'm Miki, welcome to our home."

"A handsome couple," Cole said, turning to face his hostess. "Thank you, nice of you to open up your home this way."

"We would do anything to advance the Kingdom. How long have you been a believer?" Miki said, turning her head in a slight angle.

"I'm not sure you would call me a believer. I'm Cole Sage. I'm a columnist with the *Chronicle*.

"Oh, you will be," Mini said, entering the room. "We were Radical Berkeley Atheists until we heard Jesse. Then it was like we could see, taste, smell, and nearly touch the Truth. You'll see."

"It seems like quite a jump from not believing, to having a man over for dinner who claims to be God," Cole inquired.

"Not so much a jump, Cole, as it was a step in the right direction." Miki giggled at her own joke and Mini joined in. "Come join the group."

Down a short hallway, Cole could hear laughing. He took in as many of the pictures lining the hall as he could as the twins led him to a large dining area.

"Everyone, this is Cole. He will be joining us for dinner." Mini offered.

Cole nodded and gave a variety of greetings to those around the table.

"You made it," Skeeter said. Cole detected a slight challenge in Skeeter's tone.

"I've never been one to pass up a dinner invitation."

"Mr. Sage is a journalist. He's here at my invitation. He's just going to hang out with us for a bit and hopefully dispel all those rumors of secret handshakes, animal sacrifice, and orgies." Skeeter's attempt at humor bore a razor-sharp edge that reinforced Cole's earlier impression.

Jesse Monday stood and offered Cole his hand. "Skeeter's sense of humor tends to be a shade on the nasty side, Mr. Sage. I hope your time with us will be productive. We have nothing but love for you and want you to feel you are one of us."

"Please call me Cole. I appreciate this opportunity to get to know you a little better and meet some of your friends."

"Thank you for not calling them disciples," Jesse said warmly.

Skeeter indicated an empty seat between a well-dressed man and a blonde woman of about fifty, with thick glasses, dressed in a flowing multi-colored tent of a dress.

"Soup?" Miki said brightly as she entered the room with a large china tureen and started it around the table. Seconds later, Mini brought several baskets of bread to the table.

"I'm Katherine," the woman began. "I hope you'll see we are not some oddball bunch of misfits. I teach at the Art Institute, raised Catholic, frequent non-attender. Sid there," indicating the man to Cole's left, "is a podiatrist. Skeeter, you've met. Lois is his, well, we're never quite sure what their relationship is, makes things exciting. Rebecca and Oscar are married and own a furniture store in Hayward. Let's see, the fellow next to them," she paused. "Excuse me, what was your name again?"

"I'm Mike."

"What do you do, Mike?" Cole asked.

"Bartender. No permanent gig. Kind of on-call at a couple different places."

Cole nodded. Mike took a spoonful of soup.

"Next to him is Barb, she's just Barb. Not sure what she does, and at the end of the table are Augie and Kyle. They are ministry support staff. And that, my new friend, is the lot of us." Katherine reached for a bread basket.

The conversation was tepid. It could have been a dinner party in a million homes, with ten million ordinary, slightly dull people. The food was nothing special; vegetable soup, tossed greens with a vinaigrette dressing, roast chicken with herbs, baby red potatoes, and green beans. For dessert, peach cobbler. Ice water and iced tea were served with dinner, coffee with dessert.

There was no talk of miracles or sermons. Kids, jobs, real estate, and politics commanded most of the conversation. It wasn't a case of the faithful sitting at the master's feet, it was just dinner.

On the few occasions Jesse took the floor, nothing was said of any particular depth, and for the most part, Cole found him to be as dull as his guests.

Try as he may, Cole couldn't get anything more than, "I was lost but now I'm found" out of the folks around him. Being the silent observer was easy in this company and there was no compulsion to move the conversation along. At one point, as Cole searched the faces of the dinner guests, his eyes met Jesse's. The gaze was unblinking. The others continued to talk and laugh, but for a long moment, Cole was locked in a sort of mental and emotional tug of war with Jesse Monday. It was as if Jesse knew the answer to a riddle. He knew Cole realized it, but to Jesse's disappointment, Cole wasn't asking.

There is something he's not telling, Cole thought. Something he wants to tell.

"Tomorrow we have the day off!" Skeeter said loudly, distracting Jesse and breaking his gaze.

"Then I'm going to turn in early." Jesse stood. "Thank you all for spending the evening with me. I draw so much energy from those I love. Mr. Sage, Cole, I hope you have seen that we are a manifestation of the blessings we have been given. No tricks, just the positive reflection of Truth's presence."

A smile and a nod were all Cole was allowed. In a heartbeat, Skeeter swept Jesse from the room. At the doorway, Jesse turned and looked at Cole. It almost felt like a cry for help. Cole dismissed it as wishful thinking.

* * *

Cole tossed the notebook on the desk. He was still pondering the look in Jesse's eyes, as real as that night at the dinner party, when Hanna tapped on the door frame.

"This is for you," Hanna said, waving an envelope at Cole.

FIVE

"What is up with this Jesse Monday guy?" Hanna stood in the doorway, a look of utter disgust on her face.

"How do you mean?" Cole replied, turning his chair from his computer.

"OK, I don't live under a rock. I may be Jewish but I get the whole Jesus thing. You think he's God's son, virgin birth, rose from the dead, all that stuff. You believe your sins are forgiven. That about right?"

"Yeah, in twenty-five words or less," Cole said, smiling.

"OK, I'm fine with all that. Not what we were taught in Hebrew school, but whatever. This Monday character to me seems like a low budget re-hash of the Jesus story. Am I right? Wasn't Jesus supposed to be the first, last and everything? Ha, I just channeled Barry White!"

"Step over here, my dear," Cole tried his best Barry White impersonation and failed miserably.

Hanna took the seat across from Cole before speaking. "What is it about him that has got all these people so upset? I simply don't get it."

"To tell you the truth, I don't either. It is the whole, the next JFK, MLK, Bobbie Kennedy, savior of the world thing. They've gotta have faith in something or someone, but I reject traditional religion-and-values-hole-in-their-soul. You're too young to remember the "Dream" of the Sixties. In your lifetime there hasn't been a hero, or cause, that the mainstream can put their faith in. Let alone see them be killed, again, and again."

"So Michael Jackson doesn't count?" Hanna grinned broadly.

"Not what I had in mind."

"Are people so weak they need that kind of a crutch?" All humor was gone from Hanna's voice.

"You're exceptionally strong. You've been through a lot in your life. You scratched and clawed your way to where you feel safe. Most people aren't that strong."

"You don't seem to need a crutch. You're smart, well read, on some days you actually have your act together." Hanna paused for effect. "So is Jesus, or God, or whatever, your crutch?"

"Nope, not a crutch, the ground beneath my feet. I've found I can't do things on my own. The sad thing is a lot of people turn to media gurus, cults, and rock stars to meet their spiritual needs, not the one who can really make a difference."

"Then we'll have to agree to disagree. I don't need anyone or anything to rely on. Never have."

"That, my dear, is your prerogative," Cole said kindly. "I've got an idea. You eat lunch with a lot of the people on our floor. You told me you were good at research, can you listen and guide without letting them know you think they're silly, weak, and being held up by a crutch?"

"I never said," Hanna said, standing.

"Oooh, touchy," Cole butted in.

"You're yanking my chain."

Cole just grinned.

"Yes! I can do this. Undercover, investigative reporter."

"Research assistant," Cole said, directing Hanna's enthusiasm back to reality.

"I'll try it today."

"Nice and easy."

"Yeah, I got it." Hanna nodded, jumping up and running back to her desk.

Cole grinned and wondered what kind of monster he'd just released on the break room. The material Carter Washington sent on Jesse Monday was scattered across the desk in little stacks that Cole alone understood.

*   *   *

"Good morning, Don. Feeling better?" Terri asked with genuine concern.

"Yeah, better, thanks."

"Busy day today. Eight-fifteen is Roger Marx. Nine is a new client, files on your desk. Ten is the budget meeting. After lunch..."

"I get it," Wiltz snapped.

He went into his office and closed the door. Before he could cross the room to his desk he heard the voice of Charlie Baranski.

"That wasn't very nice," Charlie said mockingly.

"I am having an emotional break at seeing Charles Baranski dead. I know that." Wiltz leaned his head back and spoke to the ceiling. "There is no voice. I have done something terrible, but I'm fine now." Wiltz took a deep breath and sighed. "Do not respond. I'll have a chat with Dr. Samuels. I just need some time to process the shock."

The sound of Baranski's laughter seemed to fill the room. "Are you kidding me? You went on a mission! You attacked the enemy," Charlie said in amazement.

"No!" Wiltz bent, putting his hands on his knees. "You are not there!"

"You're right. I'm not speaking. You're not hearing me," Charlie said sarcastically. "Get a grip! We are warriors. We don't whimper. We fight. I am alive and in a new dimension. Follow me to a final victory."

"Victory over what?" Wiltz pleaded.

"The never-ending stream of wounded, crippled warriors with their minds ripped in two. You, of all people, have to ask me that? We are sent out to fight wars the politicians have no intention of winning. We suffer, they get rich."

"We? I am one man and you are..." Wiltz's words faded as Charlie's grew stronger.

"We'll start with Vietnam. Our war. Then we will move forwards; Bosnia, Desert Storm one, two, three, whatever the hell number we're on, Afghanistan. We will fight the wars to win. We will fight it here, where it should have been fought. We are not protecting America, we're protecting oil. We will bring the war home and we will win here on our own streets."

The few feet to his desk felt like miles. Wiltz collapsed in his chair and put his forehead on his desk. In the silence of his office, Don Wiltz saw his life. The broken men that sat across his desk begging, pleading for a way to kill the demons in their heads. How many got better? Few, if any. Then they end up like Charles Baranski, or worse, they spiral into a world of depression, fear, and madness.

Could this war be won? Could I make a difference? Can I balance the scale for the grist mill of broken men and women spewed from the military grinder? The questions came rapid-fire and Wiltz physically jerked with the introduction of each new thought.

"The problem is," Charlie whispered softly, "we bring the war home. Vietnamese, the very people we lost the war to, are here in San Francisco. Our streets are teeming with scarf-wearing Muslim women, the same women who made love to the men who planted roadside bombs that blew off legs and killed our brothers. We are being choked to death by our enemies right here at home, and no one lifts a finger."

"I don't care," Wiltz said softly.

"Yes, you do, Donald, yes, you do.

"Tonight we will continue our offensive. We will..." Charles words were cut short by a tap at the door.

"Yes."

The door opened about half-way and Terri said, "Mr. Reynolds is here."

"All right. Can you hit the lights?"

A young man with a distinct limp crossed the room to Wiltz's desk with a blue file folder in his hand.

"Good morning," Wiltz offered.

"Good morning, sir," Reynolds said, offering the folder to Wiltz.

"Please have a seat. I am Don Wiltz. I will be your benefits counselor."

The parade of wounded warriors after Reynolds was non-stop. A half-hour break for lunch was Wiltz's only escape from the pain, confusion, and apprehension of the men and women assigned to him. He ate his ham and cheese sandwich from the cafeteria and tried to remember a face, one face he met with through the morning. What did he say to them? There was nothing he could bring up, nothing he remembered of their files, faces or conversations.

The last couple of Fritos dropped from the bag and hit his tray. Wiltz crumpled the bag and held it tight in his fist. The faces in the room made no sounds. Earbuds plugged in tight, phones in hand, they feverishly tapped out texts. There were no magazines, no newspapers, here and there people reviewed files as they grazed away at salads and fruit bowls.

"They're not like us, are they?" Charlie's voice was clear as if he sat across the table. "We have become a nation of bubbles, little self-contained units, unaware, and uncaring of the world around us."

"They care," Wiltz said.

"Really? Drop your fork, better yet, drop your tray. See what happens."

"That's silly."

"Is it? Drop it."

Without hesitation, Wiltz put the last few Fritos in his mouth, moved the paper plate with the second half of his ham and cheese, and his milk onto the table. He slowly moved the tray to the edge of the table. Little by little, he pushed it over the edge. His movements were almost undetectable. The tray tilted, and with a little more encouragement, toppled over the edge onto the floor.

The heads in the cafeteria didn't turn. The iPods played on, and heads bobbed in rhythm. The texters didn't miss a stroke, and a couple of the file readers shifted in their seats but didn't look up.

"Told ya," Charlie said with a chuckle. "We don't exist."

Wiltz bent over and picked up the tray. He put the tray back on top of the table with a clang. He was alone in a room full of people. Silent, focused, oblivious people, unaware of his moments, or the noise he made. Is he the tree that fell in the forest? Did he really make any noise if no one heard him?

"They are slaves waiting to be captured by the strangers in our land; Muslims, Mexicans, Asians, and the criminal black armies of the ghettos. We must sound the alarm, Donald, you and I."

Wiltz covered his mouth with his hand. "I'm not the one to help you. One man can't change anything."

"Edison brought the world out of darkness. Steve Jobs gave these sheep their distractions, Jesus changed the entire world; Just men, just an idea, just a willingness to try. You, Don Wiltz, can change this city. You can start a fire that will change the nation."

"You must leave me alone, Charlie," Wiltz said into the palm of his hand.

"Put your hand down. We already proved you are invisible."

"I wish I believed what you're saying."

"Do you remember how good it felt to see that Viet Cong-infested nail shop go up? Imagine how it will feel to see whole sections of the enemy's encampments aflame. We can do this." Charlie's fervor seemed to echo from the walls.

"I wish I believed you," Wiltz said loudly, testing his non-existence.

"Tonight I will make you a believer. The warrior will rise, a movement will ignite, and we will begin the reclaiming of America. You'll see."

Without looking around, Wiltz stood and picked up his sandwich. He didn't return his tray or throw away his trash. He walked out unnoticed. Charlie was right, he was invisible.

Appointment after appointment, Wiltz gave his presentation in a pre-programmed robotic stupor. The scheduling meeting went without him saying a word. At three o'clock Terri brought him a cup of coffee and a chocolate chip cookie.

"I made these last night. Thought you might like an afternoon pick-me-up."

"Thanks." Wiltz looked at the secretary and felt a wave of embarrassment come over him. "Sit down, Terri," Wiltz motioned to the chair in front of him. He took a bite of the cookie and smiled. "How long have we worked together?"

"Almost two years," Terri replied.

"Do you think we do any good?"

A frown took the joy from Terri's face and there was hurt in her eyes.

"I'm sorry I snapped at you earlier. You're a very nice person. You have to be, to put up with me." Wiltz forced a smile.

"That's never been a problem." Terri blushed as she let the slightest hint of her feelings for her boss show. "I like my job, and you are great to work for."

"But," Wiltz sighed. "Are we doing any good? These young, and not-so-young, men and women come in here and are in such desperate need of help. No, hope is a better word, and I just don't think I have what they need." He sat up a little straighter. "Are we just part of the machine that ground them up and spat them on our doorstep?"

"Oh, Mr. Wiltz, Don, you are so wonderful with our clients. I know it must be an emotional drain to deal with pain and suffering all day long, but you do make a difference. Truly." Terri's response was kind of a love letter to him coded in comforting words.

She really is lovely, Wiltz thought. "Sometimes, I just feel like we are putting a Band-Aid on cancer. I mean, what do we do to give them a sense of justice? How do we extract some revenge for their pain and suffering? They are torn and their lives ruined, and for what? What was their sacrifice for?"

"I've never heard you talk like this before."

"I think I have come to an understanding of how futile it all is." Wiltz stared at Terri but she couldn't bear to look at him.

"You are the best counselor we have. Your clients appreciate you so much; they say so all the time."

"I wish I believed I was helping." Wiltz took another bite of cookie, but he didn't look at Terri. "I think maybe Charlie Baranski was right."

"No, Don, he killed himself! Don't talk like that, you scare me," Terri said with genuine concern.

"Not that. I meant about us losing. He was right." Wiltz took another bite of cookie.

Terri stared at Wiltz, completely baffled by what he was saying. "Why don't you let me cook you dinner tonight? You really seem like you need someone," Terri cleared her throat softly, "Someone who cares about you."

Wiltz was a bit taken aback by this declaration of feelings from his secretary. He was attracted to her; he would love a woman in his life. "That would be nice," Wiltz replied with a gentle smile and a nod.

* * *

"Hanna Day, super sleuth reporting, sir!"

Cole turned to face a smiling Hanna who simply beamed with her own self-congratulations.

"This ought to be good."

"Anybody here seen my good friend Jesse? Can you tell me where he's gone? Up over the hill, with Abraham, Martin, and John." Hanna laughed at her attempt at singing before continuing. "Most of the people in the break room making such a fuss over the death of Jesse Monday never heard him speak, never attended a rally, a meeting, or whatever you call it. As far as I could determine, they have no idea what he said, believed or preached."

"And exactly how did you come to this astute observation?" Cole prodded.

"For starters, I was sitting next to a woman who looked like somebody sat on her canary. So, in my most concerned counselor voice, I asked if there was anything wrong. She told me she was just upset over the death of Jesse Monday. I asked her if she was a follower. No, she was a Catholic. Had she attended one of his meetings? Nope. About that time we were joined by three women from the sports desk. I asked them if they were as upset at my new friend. 'Oh, yes. He will be really missed.'

"Of the three women, one was a true believer. Up until his death, she was trying to get her co-worker to go see Jesse. She could really talk the talk. Truth, truth, and more truth. I couldn't seem to get a clear picture of what 'Truth' was exactly. The long and short of it was they were all Raiders fans until the Niners went to the Super Bowl."

"So your conclusion is a large shot of mass hysteria with a bandwagon chaser?"

"You know how when a rock star dies and they suddenly are number one in the charts, and the week before they couldn't get arrested? Same thing." Hanna was convinced in her findings. Cole wasn't so sure.

"Let's see if you can get me in touch with Jesse Monday's right-hand man. His name is Skeeter Evans. See if he remembers me and ask for a face-to-face."

* * *

Claw Hammer Hardware was a small, old-fashioned, nuts and bolts hardware store. Rows and rows of molly bolts, hinges, clamps and a million and one things you need once or twice in life. When you do, they are there for you. The place is poorly lit and cluttered. The staff knew their inventory and where every lynchpin, rubber faucet washer, and eighth-inch drill bit is hiding and how much it will cost. Wiltz was completely out of his element.

"Help you, sir?" asked a man in his sixties wearing a Claw Hammer t-shirt.

"Yes. I need a few things for a project I'm working on. I need two large funnels, with big what-do-you-call-them, the part you put in the tank?" Wiltz asked.

"The spout?"

"Yeah, spout. Four feet of two-inch tubing," Wiltz paused and tried to remember what else he needed.

"Don't forget the duct tape." The sound of Charlie's voice seemed to come from over Wiltz's shoulder.

"Some duct tape," Wiltz said softly.

"You makin' a Beer Bong?"

"A what?"

"The kids from the college are always coming in for funnels and tubes. They put the tube in their mouth and pour beer down the funnel. Hell, we used to chug-a-lug. This seems quicker!" The hardware man laughed loudly and slapped Wiltz on the back. "Let's get you some tubing."

A few minutes later Wiltz boarded the bus and made his way home. On his kitchen table, he assembled the parts he bought. One funnel was inserted and duct taped into the tubing. The other funnel Wiltz smashed to make a wide thin exit for fluid. He smiled at his resourcefulness and laid it to the side.

Shortly before six, he pulled up in front of Terri's apartment building. He showered, shaved and put on fresh clothes. It was several years since he'd been on a date. He wasn't sure if this counted, but he was excited just the same. At the bottom of the stairs, he paused and took a deep breath.

"Well, so where do you do think you're going?" Wiltz was jolted by the sound of Charlie's voice.

"Not now, Charlie," Wiltz muttered.

"Then when? What is it exactly you think you're going to do with that woman anyway?"

"We are going to have dinner," Wiltz said, holding his head up proudly.

"She has a lot more than Chicken Divan on her mind tonight. You are the main course and she wants you served up on fresh sheets!" Charlie laughed wickedly.

"No, she doesn't!"

"You are such a fool. She drools all over you; Brings you cookies, aspirin. 'Are you All right?' It makes me puke!" Charlie's mocking was almost more than Wiltz could stand.

"If she does offer me love, I accept!" Wiltz said, taking the first stair.

"My legs may have been worthless, but I could do the deed. You've peed sitting down for over forty years. Is this your chance to reclaim the manhood the Gooks shot off?" Charlie burst into a fit of fiendish laughter. "She wants a stallion, not a gelding!"

Don Wiltz threw his hands over his ears and from his throat rose a guttural soul-shredding cry. He spun about and ran to his car. He sat for several minutes in the parking lot, sobbing, swearing, stomping, and pounding the steering wheel.

"Let's go home," Charlie whispered gently.

After taking off his new shirt and splashing his face repeatedly, Don Wiltz microwaved a chicken pot pie and laid out two of Terri's cookies for dessert. Shortly after eight o'clock, Wiltz went to bed. He set his alarm clock for two a.m.

As he loaded the tube and funnel in his trunk, Charlie spoke for the first time in hours. "Don't forget to buy gas."

"I won't forget," Wiltz snapped.

"Cranky after our nap?" Charlie mocked.

"Leave it," Wiltz said sourly.

"Yes, sir. Just trying to help."

Gasco is a twenty-four-hour mini-mart with six gas pumps. It is dirty, half the hoses have been cut and the clerk sits behind two inches of bullet-proof glass. The appeal to Wiltz is the video camera was shot out months ago and never replaced. He would never have known about the place if one of his clients didn't work there. The man joked that "if he had been that pro-tected in Afghanistan he would still have two arms".

Five gallons of gas sure pump slowly, Wiltz thought as he watched the dials rotate. He paid for the gas in cash and tried not to make eye contact with the attendant. He needn't have bothered; the attendant was more interested in the infomercial on the snowy 12-inch TV above the counter than the sale.

The Happy 3 Nail Salon was cordoned off with yellow tape. One front window was covered with ply-wood. The carbon black of the fire showed above the wood. On the other side, Wiltz could see the sky through the roof. Wiltz kept rolling past.

The street was dark and only a few cars were parked here and there. Wiltz rounded the block, trying to decide who posed the greatest danger.

"They can't eat, they can't fight. Let's starve them out. Like my guys used to do in the tunnels."

Charlie's voice was an unwanted interruption. Wiltz was feeling in charge and ready for the attack.

"I'm one step ahead of you," Wiltz said. "Pho is on the menu for tonight!"

Wiltz tuned off his lights as he entered the alley. The only light came from the reflection of a street lamp bouncing off the few remaining windows in the derelict warehouse that ran nearly the length of the alley. The back doors of the shops were protected by security doors. Some were blocked by broad steel cross-bars, chains, and heavy padlocks. The merchants of this block were firmly committed to stopping break-ins.

To be able to reach an access ladder, Wiltz parked his car close to the wall. The ladder was installed with a six-foot metal covering; the idea being that would-be climbers couldn't get past the smooth, slick surface. The padlock, if there ever was one, was gone. The ring it once went through was drawn back and the protective cover took Wiltz only seconds to swing open.

He climbed on the roof of his car to reach the ladder. Quickly realizing he couldn't climb the ladder and carry the five-gallon gas can, Wiltz put his belt through the handle of the can and buckled it. He put the strap over his shoulder and draped his tube and funnel around his neck. The weight of the gasoline made climbing difficult, but within a couple of minutes, he was on the roof.

The cool air felt good as Wiltz filled his lungs in an attempt to catch his breath. From the rooftop, it seemed he could see for miles. As he approached the center of the roof above Viet Pho, something was not right. He looked down the length of the building in both directions. It seemed every space had an air conditioning unit except this one. For a moment he panicked.

The plan that seemed so smart and simple was falling apart. Should he choose another business?

"What's your problem, soldier?"

"I don't need your help, Charlie!"

"That's not very nice, we're partners."

"I know what I'm doing."

"Doesn't look like it from here." Charlie laughed heartily.

Wiltz frantically looked around the roof. Why was there no air conditioner? He began moving to the center of the building.

"Whatcha lookin' for?"

"That!" Wiltz, said proudly, pointing at a blue tarpaulin on the roof.

In the spot where the air conditioner must have been was a four-by-six-foot sheet of blue plastic tarp securely duct-taped to the roof. Wiltz set the gas can and tubing on the roof and began tearing back the tarp.

"You see?" Wiltz asked.

"I see two big holes in the roof. So?" Charlie said sarcastically.

"It's all I need."

In an instant, Wiltz removed the cap of the gas can and was pouring gasoline down the hole on the left. After a few moments, he righted the can and shook it, then poured a bit more. Satisfied he'd reached the half-way point of his fuel, he moved to the other hole. It wasn't long before the can was empty.

Wiltz moved the empty can to the edge of the building. He returned to the air duct holes in the roof. For a long moment, he stood smelling the gasoline wafting through the air. He took a box of wooden matches from his jacket pocket. Removing three matches he held them close together and struck them on the side of the box. In one fluid motion, Wiltz bent down and stepped back, dropping the matches down a hole.

An orange pillar of flame burst from the hole. He quickly took three more matches out of the box and struck them.

"Fire in the hole!" Wiltz laughed and dropped the matches.

This time he didn't wait to see the flames. He felt the heat on his back and neck as he ran to the edge of the building. Looping his belt around his neck and then the unused tube and funnel, he moved quickly down the ladder and was in his car in less than a minute.

The car bounced hard in the gutter as Wiltz left the alley and turned onto the dark street. He drove without his lights as he turned the corner and slowly cruised towards Viet Pho. Unlike the nail shop, the fire in the small restaurant was raging by the time he reached it. Three car lengths past the blaze, the front windows of the noodle shop blew out. Don Wiltz smiled and accelerated.

SIX

"Tell me again what we got her?"

"Cole, I'm ashamed of you!" Kelly scolded.

"You wrapped them before I saw them, I'm lacking clarity."

"Clarity?"

"That's right. I'm not quite clear on what we got her," Cole said, looking down at the two packages Kelly held.

"I got her two tops and leggings. You got her the Sing-a-long-Disney video game."

Before Cole could respond, the front door flew open and Jenny came bounding out onto the porch and jumped to the sidewalk just in front of her maternal and paternal grandparents.

"Hola, abuelo" Jenny squealed, jumping up into Cole's waiting arms.

"Hola, mi princesa! Feliz cumpleaños!" Cole said, giving Jenny a big kiss on the cheek.

"Hola, abuela!" Jenny suddenly lunged in Kelly's direction and threw her arms around her neck. Cole nearly dropped her. "Are those for me?"

"You are the only birthday girl I see!"

"Hola, papa," Erin said from the top step. "Jenny, calm down!"

"Hola, anciano!" Ben chuckled.

"Obviously the bilingual school is working out," Kelly laughed.

"For who, is the question. Hi, Mom!" Ben said, stepping forward to give Kelly a peck on the cheek.

Once inside, things calmed down a bit. Jenny took Kelly into the kitchen to show her the birthday cake sitting on the counter.

The birthday dinner was fast and easy. Jenny planned the menu which included taquitos, bagel bites, raw broccoli and ranch dip, and frozen yogurt.

"I got a call from my friend Christine today," Kelly began. "She's the one that bought the small winery in Paso Robles. I've been telling her I would come and visit for ages. Anyway, I'm going down tomorrow to help label and box their first offering."

"What about Easter?" Erin asked.

"I'll be back on Saturday afternoon. But here's the thing. I am babysitting my neighbor Charla's goldfish while she's on a cruise. So, Cole..." Kelly gave him her most beguiling smile.

"Will I feed the fish?" Cole grimaced.

"Could you?"

"I suppose so." Cole was less than enthusiastic in his response.

Presents opened and ice cream eaten, Jenny was off to bed. Kelly and Cole stayed another forty-five minutes. The drive to Kelly's was chatty and full of good-hearted teasing. The couple enjoyed a place in their relationship where they were very comfortable with each other. Not that there weren't surprises, but periods of silence were no longer awkward, and their mature affection was not driven by the raging hormones of the young.

Sometimes Cole just delighted in the sound of Kelly's voice and her gentle spirit. The wit and quick mind that first drew him to her was just the key to opening an amazing intellect that never ceased to invigorate Cole. Tonight was no different. As they moved through traffic and toward the bridge, music playing softly, Kelly spoke eloquently about her faith and her concern for people's willingness to follow a man like Jesse Monday. She wasn't judgmental, just bewildered, and Cole found her knowledge of the charismatic gurus in her lifetime, from Jim Jones, David Koresh, and L. Ron Hubbard, to Sun Myung Moon and José Luis de Jesús to be amazing.

She spoke of each one in turn and how they twisted the Bible and the teachings of Jesus to enslave, bilk, and in too many cases, aid in the deaths of their followers. Cole agreed. He was baffled by people's willingness to give themselves to a leader to the point of abandoning reason and their own emotional, spiritual and financial freedom.

Cole was prepared to walk Kelly to the door of her floating home when she leaned over and gave him a slow kiss, her palm gently caressing his cheek, then without a word, hopped out of the car.

As she turned before closing the door she smiled and whispered, "I love you, sweetie. Big day tomorrow. I'll call you." With that, the door closed and she made her way briskly to the ramp to the pier.

"So much for cuddling on the couch." Cole smiled and shook his head.

Cole's morning was delightful, from the perfect temperature of his shower, the homemade ham, egg, and cheese sandwich, the four-star mocha, even the traffic lights on the way to work were cooperative. The sun was shining and the mix-disc in his CD player was just one more sign that the day held nothing but good things ahead.

When he arrived at his office there was no sign of Hanna, nothing unusual there. Her jacket was draped on the back of her chair, so she was in the building somewhere. Continuing his run of morning bliss, there were only two messages on his desk, neither one of which bore the signs of derailing his mood.

"Happy Monday morning!"

"Yes, indeed!" Cole said, looking up to find Hanna in the doorway with two large Styro cups.

"I'm stepping out to the skinny end of the limb here, but I made you a mocha. I have to say the recipe for my last boss's morning coffee was easier; black, two fingers of Bourbon. Cocoa, creamer and Sweet'N Low is an entirely different kind of mixology."

"Wow, that's great!" Cole said, taking the cup. "Have a seat. We'll see what's on the docket for to-day." Cole took a sip from the steaming cup. "By George, I think she's got it!"

"Really?" Hanna said proudly.

"Absolutely. You're hired." Cole smiled and took another sip. "Again."

"I got a hold of that Skeeter guy," Hanna began. "What a jerk. I wasn't able to get him to commit to a sit-down, but he said he would call back when things were less hectic. For a messiah's right-hand man he sure wasn't all about goodness and light."

"He's a tough cookie. Keep on him. Give him some space but don't let him forget us. The film festival is coming up, I know it's an entertainment thing, but see if you can get me on the press list." Cole sipped the mocha, "This really is good. What about that budget packet? Did you look at it?"

"It seems that Sports is getting a pretty good increase. I guess that's what a World Series will do for you. How does Features and Editorial get a bigger cut?"

"Find Jesse Monday," Cole said flatly.

"Speaking of Mr. Monday, one of the girls I ate lunch with sent me a packet of stuff she gathered from various rallies and gatherings. I was just going through it and..."

The phone rang, interrupting Cole's new "investigator" before she could summarize her findings.

"Cole Sage."

"Cole! It is Leonard."

"Hey, buddy, what's goin' on?" Cole asked cheerfully.

"Maybe nothing."

"Nothing is always better than something," Cole said, then covering the phone, "We'll finish later." Hanna stood, saluted, and made her way back to her desk.

"This is kind of a goofy thing. This morning while two of our guys were having coffee at the end of their shift, somebody dropped a newspaper in the front seat of the squad car. Of course, nobody saw a thing." Chin cleared his throat and then continued. "There was a yellow sticky note attached to the front page. It just said, 'Have Cole Sage write the end of the story."

"What story?"

"We've had two arson fires in Little Saigon in the last four days. The sticky note was stuck to this morning's report of the second fire."

"What kind of fires?" Cole asked.

"Don't you even read your own paper?" Chin chided.

"My subscription ran out."

"Funny. The first one was a nail salon. The second was a noodle shop; different streets, but a block apart." Chin was thinking out loud.

Cole was no longer listening to Leonard Chin, he was fishing around in his trash can. Luckily, the janitors were on an every-other-day cleaning schedule. Near the bottom was the envelope, and on top of it was the crumpled yellow letter.

"Tell me about the note again," Cole said.

"Not much to tell. It was just a few words on a sticky note written in black felt tip pen. '*Have Cole Sage write the end of the story.*'"

Cole smoothed out the crumpled piece of legal paper on his desk. "I'll fax you something. Hold on a second." Cole covered the phone. "Hanna, please fax this to this number," Cole called out a number from his Rolodex.

Hanna grabbed the crumpled sheet and scurried from the room.

"I got a weird letter. I thought it was just another screwball rant and tossed it. This doesn't sound like a coincidence."

"I don't believe in coincidence," Chin replied.

"Got it yet?"

"Yeah, here it comes. Hold on."

"I don't imagine there is any relationship between the two torched businesses," Cole continued.

"No, but there is with these two notes. It's the same handwriting."

"Were there fingerprints on the sticky note?" Cole asked.

"No, and I bet a buck there won't be any on this one either."

"Send somebody to pick it up and you can dust the letter."

"Why don't you just bring it with you?" Chin asked.

"Where?"

"To the fire site," Chin answered. "You're coming to get the story, right?"

"No."

"What do mean, no?" Chin said in disbelief.

"I'm in the middle of a really big assignment. I can't just drop it to follow a nut case."

"Yeah, but it appears that you are part of this," Chin insisted.

"What, because some nut job wants me to write the story? Been there, done that. No thanks."

"You mean the guy with the bomb that wasn't a bomb? I got a lot of mileage on that one, telling people we were friends. I even told people I taught you the pencil thing," Leonard Chin said, trying to get a reaction from Cole.

"Geez, Chin."

"Just giving you a hard time. Seriously though, there's no way you can't take a couple of days and lend a hand? You could get into your cop wanna-be mode." Chin was pulling out all the stops.

"So, did Margaret Cho die and they need a new Asian comedian?" Cole gave back as good as he was getting.

"All right, I tried. I'll send somebody over to pick up your letter. I'll add it to the file."

"OK, keep me up to date."

"No, you made your choice."

"Funny," Cole grunted.

"Later," and with that, Chin was gone.

You think Matt Drudge has these kinds of problems? Cole thought. He must admit his heart really wasn't in the Jesse Monday story. The guy's been dead four days. That means if they were hatching up some kind of a resurrection scheme they were a day late.

Cole worked through lunch, putting together a framework for this feature on Jesse. The obituary was pretty straightforward. Chuck Waddell wanted closure. Did Chris Ramos follow a fake, a false prophet? Cole knew Waddell well enough to know he was hoping for a "stairway to heaven" story. Cole knew he wouldn't get that.

Two o'clock came and went and the need for fresh air, food or both was the wall Cole hit.

"I'm going to go grab a bite," Cole said, passing Hanna's desk.

A brisk breeze met Cole on the sidewalk. He took a deep breath and decided on a falafel wrap for lunch. With no cars coming, Cole darted across Mission and made his way to the light on 5th. It was after the lunch rush and it should be quiet. The sun seemed to make the sky a deeper shade of blue and the awnings on Soma just a bit more burgundy. Cole took another deep breath as he walked towards the corner.

"Don't turn around," a voice said as Cole felt a hard object shoved against his back.

"OK, who is it?" Cole said sarcastically as he began to turn.

"I will shoot you. I am invisible. No one seems to know I exist or pays any attention to what I do. They are too busy on their cell phones." The voice was hard and showed no sign of humor.

"Right here in broad daylight? With cops and city workers everywhere? Right." Cole stopped abruptly. "What do you want?"

"Keep walking and turn left at the corner."

"I want to go to Soma's," Cole popped off.

A hard blow to the back of the head made Cole's vision sparkle.

"Just in case you want to continue with the funny comments." The voice behind him seemed to pulsate in Cole's ears.

"All right. I get it." Cole stammered as he turned to cross back over Mission.

In front of the Mint building, a city crew diverted traffic. They removed a manhole cover and were running a large blue cable down the hole. The canvas tent all but blocked the visibility up Mission Street. There was no one in front of them and Cole felt the pressure of the gun in his back ease.

A few yards up 5th Street, the voice said, "Cross."

Cole obeyed, stepped off the curb, and walked toward the old Mint building.

As they passed a bus shelter, the voice behind him said, "Sit down."

One of the Plexiglas panels was out of the back of the shelter. "Keep your eyes on the *Chronicle* building," the voice commanded.

Still aching from the blow to the head, Cole complied silently. The man moved around behind Cole and put the cold steel of the gun to the back of Cole's neck.

"What do you want?" Cole asked harshly.

"Just to have a chat."

"We could have done that at Soma's over lunch."

"I don't think you are taking this seriously." The voice was followed by a sharp rap to the top of Cole's head. "I have something to say, and you're making it difficult. It took me quite a while to realize that you were the Sage I met in 'Nam. The piece you did a while back on the treatment of aging veterans in the Bay Area clicked it in place."

"Do you need help? I met some good people doing that story. I can put you in touch. This way is not going to get you far." Cole spoke with a direct firmness.

"My problems are my own. My concern is for America. My friends died in Vietnam. Others lost their sons in the Middle East. Now these people are everywhere you look. We have lost the wars and the victors have invaded our city. I am doing something about it. I will continue to burn their nests until the last one is gone. Little Saigon, Little Bangkok, what is next, Little Basra? There are no more Americans. Illegals get welfare, food stamps, and free medical. Vets are left dying in cold hallways." The man behind Cole paused.

"Tell him it is his responsibility to tell the truth and rid the city of this vermin." For the first time, Charlie spoke to Don Wiltz.

"I will. I will," Wiltz said aloud.

"Will what? Cole questioned.

"Nothing, never mind. Your job is to tell the story."

"How's that?" Cole asked.

"You were a condescending smart ass in Saigon. You haven't changed, just got old. I almost didn't recognize you. Had to look you up on Google to make sure." Wiltz was interrupted again.

"Enough with the family reunion. Let's get this done." Charlie was yelling this time.

"All right!" Wiltz shouted. "Tonight the fire will blaze again. You have friends in the police, I'm sure. In the morning, call them. Then write the reason for the fires. Demand the removal of all enemy combatants and their offspring from America."

"Look. What's your name?" When there was no response, Cole continued, "We both know that's never going to happen. Do you really think burning down a few businesses is going to make the government round up people and deport them? Really? You'll be caught, and you will be punished. Let's do this the smart way. Turn yourself in. No, better yet, I'll go with you. Then I'll interview you and tell your side of the story. Then..."

"Do you think I'm an idiot?" Wiltz screamed.

"No, I think you need help," Cole said very calmly, but firmly.

"He thinks you're nuts! Kill him. Show him, show him that you may not have any balls but you are strong and will get the job done!" Charlie's voice exploded in Wiltz's head.

"Killing him will not get done what I want done!" Wiltz growled.

"Tell your friend that enough people have been killed." Before Cole could start his next sentence the *Chronicle* building turned white, bright red, and then everything went black.

The next thing Cole knew he was looking up at a Muni Bus driver, a police officer, and a paramedic.

His wrists were zip-tied to the bus bench and a twelve-inch section of one-inch pipe was lying in his lap.

"Can you tell me your name, sir?" the muscular African American policeman asked.

"Sage, Cole Sage."

"You're OK," the paramedic said reassuringly. "You've taken a nasty blow to the head."

"Three," Cole replied.

"How's that, sir?" the officer interrupted.

"Three blows to the head."

"Let's get these off of you." The policeman cut the zip-tie on Cole's right wrist. "Can you tell me what happened?"

Cole's head felt like it was filled with crude oil as he tried to process what did actually happen. His wrist stung as the second zip-tie was cut loose. The aching in his neck and shoulder eased a bit as he rotated on the bench.

"It wasn't a gun," Cole said, picking up the section of pipe. "A guy stuck this in my back as I approached the corner over there. Said he was happy to shoot me so I played along. I don't think he was on the phone, but he kept answering, arguing actually, with somebody."

"Did he take anything?"

Cole reached for his wallet. "Doesn't appear so."

Through the thumping throb of the knot on his head, Cole decided to keep the exact content of their conversation to himself for a while. He needed to get back across the street and call Leonard Chin.

"Got an aspirin?"

The paramedic pulled off the blood pressure cuff and smiled at Cole. "Everything but."

"Then I need to get back to work."

"I really think an x-ray might be a good idea."

"What, of my head? Already did that, it's empty."

"Where's work, sir?" the policeman asked.

"Across the street." Cole pointed to the *Chronicle* building.

"You're the columnist!" the police officer said brightly. "My wife is a big fan of yours. Wait 'til I tell her you got zip-tied to a bus bench. You want my name for the story?"

"I think I'll just keep this one to myself," Cole replied with a grimaced smile.

"That's too bad, would've been nice for the scrapbook."

"I tell you what, Officer Marcum." Cole caught a quick look at his brass name-plate, "If I do write the story, you're in."

"You're all right!" Officer Marcum beamed.

The paramedic zipped his duty bag closed. "I still think you should get an x-ray."

"I just may do that." He knew he wouldn't but he figured it was the easiest way to end the conversation.

"If I don't go to the corner, are you going to give me a jaywalking ticket?"

"I'll do you one better. I'll walk you across myself," Marcum offered. "I usually reserve that kind of treatment for little old ladies, but you're looking a bit peaked."

"You are a gentleman," Cole countered, once again trying to manage a smile.

"That was quick," Hanna said without looking up.

"Lost my appetite," Cole replied as he closed his office door.

Cole's fingers gently felt the two lumps and tender spot on his head. He didn't wanted to examine his injury while with the paramedic. He thought the farther removed he appeared from the pain, the quicker he could get back to his office and the phone, but the pain was growing more pronounced by the minute.

Scrounging around in his top desk drawer, he found a bottle of aspirin. Never one to read labels or follow directions, Cole took four and rinsed them down with the inch of cold mocha still sitting on his desk. The stiffness in his neck and shoulders eased a bit as he rotated his head from side to side. He buried his face in the palms of his hands and gently rocked with the throbbing beat in his head.

Are there more screwballs than there used to be? Cole thought as he replayed the strange encounter. What did he said about Vietnam? If there was a connection, it was one-sided because Cole neither recognized the voice or the reference. And what was the rant about enemies in the street? Cole's head continued to pound.

The face of his watch was blurry but Cole could still see that it was after four-thirty, as he opened one eye and peeked through his finger.

"It was such a nice morning," Cole mumbled as he gently leaned his head on the back of his chair.

The pounding rhythm of Cole's throbbing head eased slightly with the pressure of his forearm across his eyes. A stream of thoughts and memories seemed to swirl and mix into an inky swamp as Cole fell asleep.

Like a diver coming back to the surface, Cole burst from the tar-thick slurry of sleep to the quick rapid knock on his door.

"Are you spending the night?" Hanna asked brightly.

Cole blinked and wiped his eyes. "I must have fallen asleep."

"From the wall-rattling snoring, I'd say about two hours ago."

"You must have needed it."

The blows to the head took more of a toll on Cole than he thought. Maybe I should have gone for an x-ray, was a recurring thought. He was sure he was concussed. Home sounded really good.

"I'm feeling pretty rough," Cole said, standing. "I'll see you tomorrow."

"Cole, you have blood on your collar!" Hanna cried as he swept past her on his way out.

"Tomorrow," was all he said.

The cool crisp air of the parking garage snapped Cole from his groggy post-nap blur. The throbbing in his head was now just a slow steady ache.

"Oh, crap, I forgot those stupid fish," Cole grumbled, opening the door of his car. *I'll do it tomorrow*, he thought, unlocking the car door.

As he bent to get in the car it wasn't quite enough and he hit his head on the doorframe.

"Ugh! I give up." Cole groaned, placing his palm on his fourth blow to the head.

Maybe it was the throbbing in his head. Maybe it was aggravation at having to drive all the way to Kelly's to feed a bunch of silly fish. Maybe it was just the routine of leaving work just like any other day that kept Cole from noticing the gray late-nineties Mazda pull away from the curb as he exited the garage.

Don Wiltz spent the afternoon patiently waiting for Cole Sage to leave the *Chronicle* building. He passed the time listening to KKSF News Talk radio and carrying on a long conversation with Charlie Baranski. He left the car only once to relieve his aching bladder in the alley. Wiltz only spent a few months in combat before being assigned to the press office, but his time in the jungle taught him to wait. He found a sense of tranquility in waiting. Sitting perfectly still, relaxed and finding the quiet place that the rest of his life lacked.

He found it amusing that he was parked only a few yards away as the police and paramedics came to Cole Sage's assistance. He watched as the lanky black policeman walked Sage across the street like a little old lady. The ambulance rolled past him and didn't even look at him. The police cruiser spun a U-turn in the street and came within feet of his car and the officer didn't even notice him. He was invisible.

Never more than a couple of cars behind, Wiltz followed Cole as he made his way to Sausalito. A delivery truck cut him off as the light turned yellow and he was stopped at the red light at the turn from Van Ness onto Lombard. For a few panicked moments, Wiltz lost sight of Cole's car. His heart pounded at the thought of losing Sage in traffic. What if he turned? What if he disappeared in traffic? Wiltz gambled an illegal lane change as the light turned to green. Darting from one lane and then another, zig-zagging through the traffic, he spotted Cole coming to a stop at a red light three car lengths ahead.

Just past the Palace of Fine Arts, a three-car collision brought traffic to a halt. From his vantage point, three cars back and one lane over, Wiltz could see Sage massaging his neck. Highway Patrol officers directed traffic, letting cars go through the bottleneck one or two at a time. Wiltz found himself stopped as the gap between him and Sage was filled by five cars.

As they approached the toll booth at the Golden Gate Bridge, Wiltz and Sage were next to each other at different booths. Wiltz pulled away first and slowed as he pretended to look at the view from the outside lane. As Sage passed him, Wiltz allowed a three-car buffer before he changed lanes.

Cole made the turn at Waldo Point Harbor, and Wiltz was directly behind him for the first time. The parking places were numbered; Wiltz took the risk and parked several spaces from Cole. He sat and watched as Sage made his way toward the houseboats before getting out of his car. Wiltz hesitated at the entry to the pier. Not wanting to get too close, he stood to the side and watched as Cole Sage entered the fourth houseboat on the right.

"Welcome home, Mr. Sage," Wiltz said angrily.

*   *   *

The smell of Kelly was like a soft kiss as Cole entered the houseboat. Everything about the place was her. Funny, he thought, I've never been here by myself, and it still feels like she could be upstairs or out on the deck. Cole smiled and walked to the counter. Kelly taped a note to the front of one of the fish tanks:

> *Thank you, sweetie, for remembering, if you are reading this!*
> *The big tank gets a teaspoon from the green can.*
> *The little tank gets ½ tsp. from the green and a ½ from the yellow.*
> *Sorry for the hassle. You will be rewarded!*
> *XOXOXOX*
> *K*

The fish seemed to know what he was there for. As the flaky fish food hit the top of the water, they surged upward like piranhas after a fat pig.

"You're a hungry bunch."

A pen was sitting on the counter next to the yellow container of fish food. Cole picked up the container, knocking the pen off the counter. Without thinking he bent and picked up the pen. As he came back up, a sharp pain shot across the back of his head, and a wave of nausea swept over him. He turned and faced the sink, sure that he would vomit.

For the first time, Cole was seriously concerned with his injury. He had been knocked out by a blow to the head before, in a car crash, from a fall from a ladder, and when he was roughed up while a prisoner in Cambodia. This time it was different.

The other fish will have to wait, Cole thought as he made his way across the room to the couch. With a swipe of his arm, he cleared the couch of all the pillows. He slowly lowered himself onto the couch and lay on his right side. He pulled up his knees and closed his eyes. Within moments he fell into a deep concussive sleep.

Don Wiltz stood for a long while at the end of the pier, watching the houseboat Cole Sage entered. Satisfied he was in for the evening, Wiltz returned to his car, popped the trunk, and stood to survey the parking lot at the pier. There wasn't a soul in sight. Wiltz removed the gas can and a box of wooden matches. He looked around one more time for signs of life, nothing. Wiltz left the trunk open, and with a swift purposeful movement made his way back to the pier and the houseboat he believed belonged to Cole Sage.

"This rids us of one more problem," Charlie spoke for the first time since Wiltz arrived at the harbor.

"He has no intention of writing our story. His obituary will be the story. If they can connect the dots," Wiltz replied.

"All this wood will make a great fire. Too bad the boats don't belong to the enemy." Charlie paused. "Walk close to the edge, less creaking."

"Finally, you have advice worth heeding. Now shut up."

Wiltz removed the cap from the gas can and tossed it into the water. Quietly, carefully and methodically he poured gasoline down the wall from about four feet off the deck. As he came to the corner he slowly moved to the sliding glass door. Glancing around the room, he didn't see Cole sleeping on the couch at first. On his second pass, he spotted Cole's white tennis shoes. Without hesitating, he crossed the back deck to the stairs. He poured gas down a pontoon vent and a bit into the gap in the sliding door to Kelly's bedroom.

Concerned with the amount of gas in the can, Wiltz left the top deck and poured gas down the deck on the side of the houseboat closest to the neighbor. Rounding the corner to the front of the houseboat, he poured a stream up the gangplank to the pier. There was still an inch or two in the gas can.

Wiltz crouched down and took several matches from the box. Striking three at once, he watched the trail of flame snake it's way down the gangplank and ignite the walls and deck. Within moments the flames covering the walls were licking the upper deck.

Trying to remain calm and walk quickly, but not excitedly, Wiltz started back to his car. As he approached Cole's car he noticed the front passenger window was down. He walked to the window, poured the remaining gas in the front seat, then tossed the can into the back seat. It only took one match to set the interior of the car ablaze.

As he started his car, Wiltz saw a woman walking a dog, her back to him. He backed out of the parking place and looked back at the houseboat. There was no smoke. A good hot fire, he thought as he pulled away. A minute later he was just another car heading for the Golden Gate Bridge.

Flames are a thing of beauty; the golds, oranges, and cleansing whiteness are one of nature's mysteries. Yet within that beauty lays the power to heat, cook, help mold, and cleanse. That same beauty also holds the power to char, destroy, and kill.

*   *   *

Kelly Mitchell created a space of beauty. Her life after the death of her husband was reshaped, revived, and began again. Her floating home was as great a departure from the large, landlocked suburban home that she could find. She buried the memories, furniture, and contents with her husband. The downsizing included a purging that helped in the healing and freed her of material encumbrances. She found freedom and energy in living on the water. Buying things for her new home released a creative and surprisingly different side of her taste than she knew existed.

Now as her new love slept on her couch, the walls burned. The drapes and bedding were aflame. The fire rolled across the floor and into the closet. Paint began to blister and run in the heat, then ignite into smoking distorted versions of themselves. Smoke swirled and floated across the floor and down the stairs from the bedroom.

The poisonous smoke and gases rose higher and higher from the floor. The couch was lost in the smoke. As the walls burned through and the fire raged unhindered, the inhalation of carbon monoxide, combined with Cole's deep sleep, lulled him into an oxygen-deprived state of unconsciousness.

As the flames and smoke rose into the azure blue Sausalito sky, Cole Sage sank further and further into the hereafter.

SEVEN

Will Rooney, owner of the houseboat two berths down from Kelly Mitchell's, awoke from a nap on his rooftop deck to the smell of acrid smoke. Then he saw the orange tips of flames.

"Kelly!" Rooney yelled, repeatedly beating on the front door. "Kelly, are you in there?"

Rooney stepped back, then rammed the door with his shoulder. The front door of the houseboat burst open onto an inferno of smoke and fire. Rooney frantically scanned the room and realized he couldn't get far inside.

His attempt to get to the back of the house was futile; the flames on the outer wall completely ignited the walkway along the right side. Without hesitating he jumped into the water and swam to the back deck. The roof above the rear deck showed evidence of the fire above. Through the glass slider, he saw Cole, lying on the sofa, his back to the glass door.

Rooney picked up a heavy flower pot on the deck and hurled it through the sliding glass door. The heat burst through the door with such a furious blast his clothing steamed. He covered his face with his arm and managed to cross the few feet to the couch and Cole.

Fearing the worst, Rooney felt for a pulse. It was weak but steady.

"Hey, wake up, fella! We gotta get you out of here!" Rooney's attempt to wake Cole was pointless—there just wasn't time.

He grabbed Cole under his arms and dragged him toward the door as a section of the ceiling collapsed near the front of the house. Outside, the deck was aflame from debris falling from above. In the distance, Rooney heard the sound of approaching sirens. He couldn't wait. There was nowhere to go but into the water. Will rolled Cole off the end of the deck into the water and quickly lowered himself in beside him.

The closest path to safety was the pontoon of the houseboat next door. Rooney grasped the collar of the motionless Cole and began kicking and paddling with his free arm, to get them the few yards to safety. They reached the pontoon at the same time the firetrucks and screaming sirens came to a stop in front of Kelly's collapsing home.

Will could feel his strength fading as he treaded water and held tight to Cole. The strenuous rescue was proving to be a lot for the seventy-six-year-old.

It took only minutes for firefighters to begin spraying down the neighboring houseboat, as they began making every effort to keep the fire from destroying more property. To their amazement, they spotted Rooney holding onto Cole and clinging to the side of the pontoon.

The fire and rescue team quickly moved the soaking pair to safety. Rooney watched, wrapped in a blanket, as the paramedics started trying to revive Cole. They determined he was suffering from severe smoke inhalation. Cole was wrapped tightly in a foil blanket; an oxygen mask covered his face as they loaded him into a waiting ambulance.

Ben Mitchell, Cole's son-in-law, was the first family member to arrive at the hospital. He came straight from USF Children's Hospital and was warmly greeted by the doctors attending Cole. Erin arrived a half-hour later with Jenny.

"It seems he has a pretty nasty concussion," the doctor informed Ben. "There are three areas of swelling and abrasion, two on the sides and a large hematoma on the top of his head. The strange thing is he has no other injuries or bruising. It's as if somebody knocked him around pretty good. Could be the arsonist knocked him out before he set the fire."

"Arsonist?" Ben couldn't help showing his surprise.

"Didn't they tell you? The houseboat he was in was torched. He's one lucky guy. An old fellow was napping a couple of houseboats down and smelled the smoke."

"My mother owns a houseboat at Waldo Point."

"The guys who brought him in didn't say where. Here's what we got. We are treating your father-in-law for the smoke inhalation first. We have him on heavy oxygen. We're waiting for the lab work to see his carbon monoxide levels. His color is pretty good, so I don't think we need a bronchoscopy. I am concerned with those head injuries, however. You know anything about any recent injuries or accident?"

"Nothing I know of. Has he woken up at all?"

"Just for a bit when we were moving him from the gurney. He said something about fish. Kind of funny, he kept mumbling, "Don't forget the fish"."

"How soon can we see him?" Ben asked.

"You have free rein around here, Doctor. Anyone else should wait an hour or so until the nurses get him settled." The doctor extended his hand, "Welcome to Marin General."

Jenny sat quietly playing a game on her iPad when Ben entered the waiting room. Erin was standing looking out the window.

"How is he?" Erin said, her voice cracking with emotion.

"He has smoke inhalation, is on oxygen, and is resting comfortably. He hasn't woken up yet. They're moving him to a room, and you can see him in about an hour." Ben smiled reassuringly and reached both arms outstretched to Erin.

"Daddy, I prayed for Grandpa, so don't worry, he'll be OK." Jenny's childlike faith was reassuring to her parents.

"Yes, he will sweetie," Erin replied, as Jenny returned to her game.

"Has your dad said anything about getting hit in the head or having an accident or anything?" Ben asked softly, not wanting Jenny to hear.

"No, why?"

"It may be nothing, but the attending physician said he had three pretty good signs of head trauma. His words, not mine," he said. "Looks like he's been knocked around."

"Where was he? What happened?"

"The fire was at Mom's."

"Have you called her?" Erin whispered.

"Yes, a few minutes ago. She's on her way back."

"What did she say?"

"All she cared about was your dad. 'Everything else is just stuff,' you know how she is," Ben tried to smile as he reassured Erin. "The house is a total loss, and your dad will be ok. That's all that matters."

"Can I see him?"

"I'm on my way in to see him. He should be awake in a bit. He will have a doozy of a headache."

"Doozy? Is that a medical term, Doctor Mitchell?" Erin smiled.

"It is a relieved son-in-law's prognosis for his wonderful wife." Ben kissed Erin on the cheek. "He'll be fine, Nurse Mitchell, truly," Ben whispered before pulling away.

Ben stood for a long moment at the door of Cole's room. It was odd to see the man he always saw as invincible in a hospital bed with IVs and oxygen.

"Hey, buddy. What brings you here?" Cole rasped, one eye still closed.

Ben crossed the room to the side of the bed and patted Cole on the shoulder. "You feel like talking?"

"That's what the cop said and I pretended to go back to sleep."

"How are you feeling?"

"If that's a doctor question, not so hot. If it's a son-in-law question that will get back to my daughter, fit as a fiddle."

"What's up with these knots on your head?" Ben asked.

Cole explained the attack on the street. He left out some of the details but gave Ben enough of the story so he understood the attack was a serious warning.

"Why were you at mom's?"

"Those stupid fish she's babysitting. They're fried fish now. Man, is your mom going to be furious." Cole paused. "What about the houseboat?"

"Gone," Ben replied sadly.

"He had to have followed me from the paper. How did I get here? All I remember is being in the water. Then the ambulance."

"They tell me the neighbor smelled smoke and got you out." Ben shrugged.

"Erin is here. You feel like company?"

"Yes, you think I can make it down to the waiting room?" Cole coughed violently.

"There you go!" Ben encouraged. "Don't be afraid to get the stuff up."

"I feel like I smoked a carton of Camels."

"Probably close. Since it appears you will not expire in the near future, I think I will get back to work. I'll check back on you later this evening."

"Tell Erin I would love to see her."

"They said an hour, so be patient," Ben replied.

"I am a patient."

"You're fine." Ben laughed as he waved from the door.

* * *

Grinds & Brews was nearly empty. A couple huddled in the corner furthest from the door and whisper-screamed at each other. To Hanna's amusement, they thought no one could hear her anger at his slovenly ways and his regret at co-signing a lease. The barista busied herself wiping down all the chrome and copper surfaces.

Hanna took a seat against the wall. She made up a tale of a doctor appointment to get to the coffee shop by nine o'clock. She called to check on Cole and he answered the phone. Grumpy and a bit grouchy, but he said he was more damaged by his hospital stay than the fire. From her vantage point, she could see the windows on either side of the door. She would be able to spot Skeeter long before he saw her.

She checked and re-checked her pen, digital recorder, and lipstick in her compact mirror. Her butterflies had all flown. Her worry about what Cole would do or think about her masquerade as a reporter was long pushed aside. She was in deep and there was no turning back now. Her only concern would be Skeeter

Evans's reaction to her sitting at the table instead of Cole.

When Hanna glanced up from her short list of questions she saw a man staring at her through the window. He looked nothing like what she envisioned on the phone. His eyes were dull, unfeeling, and devoid of emotion. He stared expressionlessly into the coffee shop. It must be him, Hanna thought.

The man in the window turned and began to walk away. Hanna ran to the door, more of a reflex than an action brought about by reasonable thought.

"Skeeter?" Hanna said, holding the door with her left hand and leaning out onto the sidewalk.

"Yeah?" Skeeter turned to face Hanna.

"I'm Hanna, we spoke on the phone?"

"Yeah."

"Wouldn't you like to come in?"

There was no effort on Skeeter Evans' part trying to hide his disgust or annoyance. He stood for a long moment, not looking at Hanna, hands shoved deep in his pockets, just gazing straight ahead.

"Where's Sage?"

"Well," Hanna hesitated, then lifted the newspaper, flashed Skeeter the headline and said, "Hospital."

"What?"

"How 'bout I buy you a cup of coffee and explain?" Hanna turned on her halogen smile and motioned for him to "come on in". He complied.

With a boxer's dexterity Hanna bobbed and weaved around any detail, or request for details

Skeeter threw at her about Cole's hospitalization. She was there to interview him, not the other way around. This was her time, and her chance, nothing was going to derail her focus.

"So what happens now?" Hanna began.

"What do you mean?"

"Jesse's gone. What will you do?"

"We continue to spread the truth of his teachings."

"Is that possible without Jesse? I mean, he was the message, wasn't he?"

Skeeter shifted in his chair and it gave a bark from scooting on the tile. He tried to seem relaxed but the rippling of his jaw muscles told an entirely different story. He took a deep breath through his nose and let it out the same way.

"Christianity seems to have done pretty well without their leader."

"Hmmm. Well, yes, it has," Hanna conceded. "But the risen-from-the-grave angle is something you don't have. I mean, where is Jesse?"

For the first time, Skeeter bristled visibly. "We don't need him."

There it was, there's nowhere to retreat from that statement. Hanna's mind raced for the perfect follow-up question. Here was more than she bargained for. If he would just not bolt; she pretended to check her notes.

Before she could formulate her next question, Skeeter continued. "The message, the vision, it was mine. Jesse was the medium, but the movement, the promotion, the program, if you want to call it that, was all my idea."

"I thought Jesse was 'God's other son' or 'Jesus for a new generation' or something. Did I get that wrong?" Hanna would rather bite her tongue out than be the first one to speak next.

Skeeter stared at Hanna through squinted eyes. This was the new beginning. Without Jesse, he was now in charge. He felt a flush of empowerment come over him. The years of guiding, polishing, coercing and playing second fiddle were over.

"Look, you people in the media will never get the big picture. This world is controlled by the spiritual. Controlling or tapping into the spiritual is given to a few vessels; Julius Cesar, Napoleon, Buddha, Muhammad, the Dali Lama, Gandhi, and although you may argue the point, Adolph Hitler. The skeptic will call it charisma, mass hysteria, marketing, or a fad. The truth is they are part of the universal spirit, a very real power, given to a very few. Jesse was a preacher, a communicator. Until he met me, he was talking to a handful of people a week. He was not part of the Power of the Air." Skeeter leaned forward and said in a softer voice, "I hope you're getting this down, you're the first to be given this truth."

"Now there's the thing that I wanted to ask about," Hanna responded. "This whole 'truth' thing, everybody says, 'Oh, Jesse shares the truth.' Or 'You need to hear the truth.' All I heard was a bunch of clever stories with an 'ah shucks' delivery. You don't have that. What is the truth, your truth?"

"The spirit knows the spirit."

"A snake eating its tail," Hanna scoffed.

"My truth is, your spirit is cold."

"It doesn't take much to figure that out. I don't buy any of this mumbo-jumbo. I'm a reporter. I'm looking for the facts and to write an article. The truth as I see it is you've found a meal ticket fleecing the sheep dumb enough to buy this fuzzy, meaningless 'Truth' nonsense." For the first time, Hanna felt in control. She was a reporter. His feet were to the fire. He had to answer. To cut and run would reinforce her skepticism.

"Truth. It's simple for those who believe."

"So are alien abductions," Hanna paused, "for those who believe. I know that the truth is admissible in court, it will set you free, and it is based in fact or reality. You can't get past 'It is what it is, everything is everything, que sera sera, and Jimmy crack corn," Hanna smiled.

"I am the Truth. I am one with the spirit world. People will come to me because what I have, Jesse Monday could never have. He was all about his little black book full of ancient stories, fabrications, and contradictions. There is a power. I surrendered to it long ago. It channels through me, it gives me insights, knowledge and as the world will see, power.

"Like Hitler?"

"You disappoint me. You just don't get it."

"I'm really trying," Hanna answered with a sincere look. "Where does this power you're talking about come from? I'm just not seeing the whole picture, I guess."

"There is a master of this world, an angel of light and such beauty it nearly blinds you. I first saw it when I was just out of high school. I never told Jesse because he would call him evil or 'the Devil.' But over time, subtly, and oh so slowly, I was able to mold Jesse's message to be more in keeping with the real power. Now is my time. I will reveal myself and I will continue to draw people to the real power of this world, a spirit of beauty and light." Skeeter's voice was as beguiling as any salesman Hanna ever heard, as smooth as any late-night, neon-lit, barroom seducer, but Hanna wasn't buying.

"So the idea of Jesse being the new Jesus?"

"Part of my plan. Let me ask you something. If you were told over the years that you were 'just like God's son', wouldn't you be flattered? If you saw droves of people coming to listen to you, wouldn't you think you had something no one else had? And wouldn't your ability to heal give you a feeling of the divine? Jesse did. His ego did.

"He never knew my team prepared the way, picked our little actors to be healed, promoted to draw the crowds, and never stopped giving him the strokes that no one could refuse. His only fault was he didn't see it. He was, in the end, a tool of the spirit I possess."

"Did you kill him?"

"Whoa, ho, ho!" Skeeter laughed. "Where did that come from?"

"Seems pretty clear Jesse outlived his useful-ness," Hanna said flatly.

"A convenience provided by the very spirit I have been talking about." Skeeter smiled, then low-ered his voice. "Adam took the apple, Lot's wife had to have a peek, and John Hinckley wanted to impress Jody Foster. You, my dear, took the opportunity while your boss was laid up to play Lois Lane. The small voice that got all those people to do what he wanted was the same voice in the back of your head that con-vinced you this meeting was a good idea."

"Murder is part of the beauty and light?"

"Liberation from this human form."

"A hard sell."

"Really?" Skeeter raised his eyebrows. "How many times have you wished the men who have hurt you were dead?"

Hanna was blindsided. Like a slap across the face with a wet dishtowel, she was momentarily stunned.

"But I had no intention of actually doing it."

"Anyone who hates a brother or sister is a murderer, St. Mark something or other. The simple fact is 'everything is everything,' as you put it. I just saw and embraced it long ago."

"So, what is the end result? For you, I mean. Why are you doing this? You're no 'soul saver.'" Hanna wanted the interview to end.

"Since I am pretty sure this will never go to print, sorry, darlin' but you're a secretary, not a re-porter. You're trying to compensate for things far deeper than interviewing me. It's in your eyes. So, I'm going to give you some truth, my truth, my only truth. Power, P-o-w-e-r. It's all I want, need or long for."

Skeeter's final words sent a chill through Hanna, and she could feel her anger welling up from deep inside her pride. He stood, tossed a ten-dollar bill on the table, and turned for the door. Her face burned hot. A thousand and one parting shots raced through her head. To her embarrassment, Hanna didn't say a word. Skeeter left the coffee shop and didn't look back.

*   *   *

"Now you've done it!" Charlie Baranski said sarcastically.

The newspaper headline seemed to scream up from the breakfast table. *Journalist Injured in Houseboat Fire.* Don Wiltz ran his fingertips over the headline.

"It wasn't even his house, you idiot."

"Shut up!" Wiltz threw his hands over his ears.

"Who's going to write the story now? How will we get our message out? You nearly killed the only one we had a chance of getting to do the story."

"I didn't know. How could I know?" Wiltz rocked back and forth in the kitchen chair.

"Maybe I chose the wrong guy for the job," Charlie snarled.

"Then go! Leave me alone," Wiltz pleaded.

"You have more missions. I will leave you soon enough. Little hole-in-the-wall shops evidently don't matter. For now, we have to think big."

"No more. I'm through." Wiltz began to weep. "I nearly killed someone."

"You're weak and disgusting. You're through when I say you're through." Charlie growled.

The phone rang and startled Wiltz. "Hello."

"Are you coming in today?" Terri asked. "It's past nine."

"I'm not feeling well. I may be in later."

"No, you won't," Charlie whispered.

"I'm sorry about..." Wiltz began.

"Maybe later," Terri cut him off.

"Still I..." the line was dead.

"There is a war to be won. We must decide on a target. You can kiss and make up later. We need something significant. Something big, that will draw attention to our cause. What do all gooks have in common, other than they squat and have slanted eyes?"

"I've warned you about your racism. This is about loss of face, not a race war."

"If I can't hate the enemy, how can I kill them?"

"We are burning property, not trying to kill anyone."

"What do all the wonderful, caring, beautiful people of Southeast Asia all have in common?" Charlie mocked.

"They're Buddhists," Wiltz replied.

"Bingo! We torch a temple!"

Wiltz stood and moved away from the table. "All Buddhists aren't part of our war," Wiltz said, his resolve coming back.

"True, but there is a Vietnamese Buddhist temple off Guerrero."

"That's too big. How can I possibly burn that?" Wiltz paced back and forth in his tiny kitchen.

"Think outside your gas can. Use what is on site."

Dressed in jeans, a gray sweatshirt, and a Giants baseball cap, Wiltz was as inconspicuous as a hundred other guys on the streets of San Francisco. The bus stopped within sight of the temple. At the bottom of the steps was a large "Welcome" sign and an invitation for lunch. Wiltz walked around to the right side of the building.

The narrow gap between the temple and the building next door was hardly wide enough for Wiltz to fit through. The back of the building opened onto a small garden with a trickling fountain and a large, bronze Buddha. Bamboo plants lined the back fences, creating a dense impenetrable wall. It was a peaceful place, and completely empty.

The left side of the building was a bit wider. Half-way to the front was a gas meter. Behind the meter was a small door that opened to a storage area and access to the crawlspace below the building. Wiltz followed the gas line to where it went up through the floor. The plumbing and gas lines in the building were old and showed signs of damage and fatigue. Wiltz spotted a workbench against one wall. A variety of tools were haphazardly scattered around the bench, among them, a large screwdriver.

Darkness nearly engulfed a wide set of shelves. They were built as part of the house and stacked to capacity with paint cans of all sizes and ages. Wiltz pulled a string attached to a small fluorescent fixture, lighting the space. Along the floor in front of the shelves were several five-gallon paint cans. One by one, Wiltz removed the lids. Some were almost full, others only held a few inches, and all were highly flammable. The cans were twenty or thirty years old and nearly all were oil-based paint.

With a methodical intensity, Wiltz popped the lids off of gallon cans and tossed them aside. At the end of one shelf were five one-gallon cans of paint thinner. Like a champagne fountain, he poured thinner in the paint cans until they overflowed and cascaded down on the next shelf. The fumes in the enclosed area were beginning to make Wiltz lightheaded. From the shelves to the door Wiltz poured a trail of thick, oily, white paint. He tossed the screwdriver back on the bench. He closed the door gently and continued on to the front of the building.

As he made his way up the steps to the front door, Wiltz saw that just like a lot of old buildings in the city, this one had been painted over and over and over. Everywhere he looked, large chips of multilayered paint had fallen off, exposing the century-old wood that lay beneath.

The front door was a bit warped and gave a screech as it opened. The entry was nothing special, a table, and a rack with reading materials. A large staircase of dark wood ran up the right wall. As he walked into what was the living room when the building was a home, the scene changed. Bright gold and red cloths draped the walls. A shrine with a large golden Buddha, flowers, and bowls of fruit filled the wall opposite. To his right was a wide arch, and in the center of the room, a long table was set with several large bowls of food, a stack of paper plates, and a basket of plastic spoons and forks. In the center of the table was a handwritten sign that read, "Help Yourself." There was no way of knowing what was upstairs; it didn't matter, the downstairs would burn fast and hot.

Wiltz left the building and walked several blocks before catching a bus for home. The plan was simple, better than he imagined, and he would return under cover of darkness to complete his mission. It was a little after twelve.

Having burned his gas container in Cole Sage's car, it needed to be replaced and filled. Wiltz strongly considered going into work on the way, long enough to apologize to Terri for standing her up, but feared the abuse he would suffer from Charlie Baranski. Wiltz tried his hardest to not even think about Charlie, for fear he would return. The peace of not having Charlie's voice in the car with him was cause for a small celebration, so Wiltz stopped at a small Mexican restaurant and ate a late lunch.

Stomach full, gas can ready, and plan set, at 2:30 Don Wiltz curled up on the couch for a nap. He slept hard, making up for the lack of rest he'd suffered since the offensive began. War was hell, and the dreams of orange napalm flames swirled and twisted with image fragments of his acts of arson. Dreams and nightmares kept Don Wiltz's nightly rest fitful and splintered.

* * *

The hallways of Marin General were silent, except for the faint humming of electronic monitoring devices. No one noticed, or paid any attention to, the tall thin figure that exited the elevator. The gray hoodie he wore hid his face, and his movements showed no sign of hesitation.

The dark-haired nurse didn't look up as a man against the far wall passed her station. Room 244 was lit only by the light coming from around the bathroom door and the glow of monitors. Cole Sage was sleeping peacefully. The hissing of oxygen and his heavy breathing welcomed his visitor as he sat down beside the bed.

The man sat silently watching Cole sleep. After a few minutes, he reached out and asked: "Are you awake?"

"If I am, you'd be the only one worried about it around here." Cole blinked several times. He looked at the man beside his bed and frantically felt around for the control buried in the blankets. As the bed rose to the sitting position, Cole said, "Skeeter?"

"In the flesh."

"What time is it?" Cole questioned, still trying to clear his vision.

"Little after three," Skeeter said.

Cole tried to clear his throat and moisten his dry tongue. Skeeter handed him the partially filled glass of water on the stand next to the bed.

"No need to talk, I just need you to listen."

Again Cole blinked and tried to shake off the cobwebs of sleep. "All right, what is it that brings you out in the middle of the night to wake a dying man?"

"You're not dying no more, smart guy."

"You got me, I'm not dying. But you have to admit a little beauty sleep wouldn't hurt me." Cole was sitting and fully awake.

"Listen up. Jesse is dead. You're a nuisance. I won't have you distracting our followers or disrupting our work."

"And exactly how am I doing that?" Cole may have been awakened abruptly but he was sure nothing of his went to print.

"Don't play dumb, the woman you sent to interview me. That was not our agreement. She has an agenda. If you want the story you should have come." His voice was angry but controlled. "I wish I hadn't talked to her, Skeeter said, almost as an afterthought.

"Buyer's remorse at three a.m.?"

"If you like. You just make sure that her stuff isn't used."

"Or what?" Cole pressed.

"We are not as unsophisticated as you want to think, Sage. We are also not some namby-pamby, turn-the-other-cheek types, either."

"Are you threatening me?"

"We can see that you are very unhappy."

"I may be in a hospital bed with all this crap hanging from my arms, but I guarantee I can still get up and kick your ass to where they put you in the next bed!" Cole's anger-burned red hot. He struggled to untangle from the bedding to throw his legs over the side of the bed.

"Oh, so who is making the threats now?" Skeeter taunted.

Cole was about to stand when a voice came from the doorway. "What is going on in here!" the night nurse bellowed.

Skeeter stood and waited for a chance to speak. The nurse wasn't having it. She blustered around the room checking monitors and getting the blood pressure cuff.

"I'll be going, Mr. Sage. You just remember what I said."

"I'll say you will," the nurse grumbled.

"Just for your information, I didn't send anybody." Cole barked. "You've given me all I need tonight."

"We will continue our conversation," Skeeter snarled, moving to the doorway.

"No need."

"Excuse me," the nurse said sarcastically, trying to get Cole back into bed.

"My number." Skeeter scribbled his cell phone number on the menu card next to the bed.

"I've had your number from the start," Cole quipped. It was too late, the man in the gray hoodie disappeared the same way he came.

*   *   *

Across the bay, Don Wiltz drove to his intended target. The street light flickered across from the temple. It made a perfect spot for Wiltz to park. The streets were empty and the lights in the buildings were out. The neighborhood was silent and the air was sweet and crisp as it gently blew into Wiltz's face.

The small access door on the side of the temple opened without a sound. It only took two matches to ignite the trail of paint he'd prepared earlier. Wiltz watched the bluish flame as it snaked its way across the floor to the shelves. There was a dull huff as the paint and thinner burst into a ball of flame. The dry split boards of the floor above seemed to embrace the fire. Quickly closing the door, Wiltz moved to the back of the building.

The unpainted boards of the back steps soaked up the gasoline like a sponge. The one-inch gap under the door and the badly bent aluminum threshold trim made it easy for the gas to enter the building. Along the right side of the building, there was no effective way to apply gas on the wall without getting splashed.

Wiltz waited until he was back in front to empty the can.

Starting at the front door, Wiltz saturated the worn and weary wooden porch with his remaining gas. He poured gas on the window ledges and under the front door. Wiltz would depend on the fire under the building to do his work for him. So as to not draw attention too early, he didn't set either the front or back porches alight.

He crossed the street and put the gas can in his trunk and got in the car. He waited for the sign of flames. Wiltz reeked of gasoline and rolled the car window partially down for a breath of fresh air. Several minutes went by; no flames were visible anywhere. He was about to go back and light the gas on the porch when he heard a low, rolling, thunder from the temple building. Within seconds the front porch went up in flames. Fire engulfed the century-old wood and paint like so much cardboard. Wiltz's mission was a success. He started the car and drove, lights off, into the darkness.

"Nice work," Charlie said.

"And without your help," Wiltz replied proudly, as he moved onto an empty Guerrero Street and turned on his headlights.

"I think we will make front page news with this one. Maybe those idiots in the police department and the dunces at the newspapers and TV news will finally put two and two together."

"You were right. This one felt good. What's next?" Wiltz said, riding the crest of adrenaline pumping through him.

"The grand finale."

EIGHT

"Hi." The soft, concerned voice of Kelly Mitchell woke Cole from his light sleep. Facing Kelly haunted Cole's sleep, dreams, and nightmares. Her home was gone and he was to blame, partially or in whole. There is a space, a sacred place; that is home, a secure refuge from the world outside. Home is a place that contains the possessions that one accumulates that, good or bad, represents where your earthly treasures lie. Scriptures say, "For where your treasure is, there your heart will be also." But we also say, "Home is where the heart is." Whatever the case, Kelly's possessions and a large piece of her heart are gone.

The dreams that have spun around the paint, fixtures, furnishings, and decorations of a home hold a piece of the owner's soul. If walls recorded the smiles, tears, laughter, and despair of the years, they would indeed play back the treasure that is a home. Kelly's houseboat was a place of grief, healing, and growth of a woman left single after years of marriage. It was a place of prayer, exploration, reading, art, film, writing and thoughts that freed her to live again.

A match, a flame, and the total destruction of the life she built were all Cole could think about. But even more than the loss of her home, Cole feared the loss of Kelly.

"Hello," Cole replied, pushing the button to elevate the bed to a more upright position. "Fancy meeting you here." His attempt at levity rang hollow.

Kelly moved to the bedside, placed her palm on Cole's cheek, and gave him a long, soft kiss.

"I am so sorry, Kell," Cole's words were cut short as Kelly placed the tips of her fingers on his lips.

"You have nothing to be sorry for. What on earth happened?"

"I was feeding the fish," Cole began.

"What? Barbecue?" Kelly quipped.

They both began to laugh. Kelly laughed until tears streamed down her face. Cole laughed, coughed, and laughed some more. The tension was broken. Kelly put down the bed rail, took Cole's hand and sat on the edge of the bed.

"Scoot over."

"I like your bedside manner." Cole raised Kelly's hand and kissed it.

"How do you feel? No Sage macho, bravado nonsense, either."

"I'm all right."

"What does that mean?" Kelly pressed.

"It means I burnt your house down, nearly died from smoke, got thrown in the water, have a bunch of needles and tubes in my arms, and frankly, I'm embarrassed as hell."

"That's better, we can work with that." Kelly adjusted herself on the bed. "Listen, about the house.

It is insured, it was meant to be a refuge after Peter's death, and it was fun. To tell you the truth I have always been afraid it would sink, so anything of any real value, things I cherished, I mean, is stored at Ben and Erin's. So it was just things. I loved it but I love you more."

Cole smiled but did not respond.

"Now, what's the story on the knots on your head?" Enter the in-charge Kelly.

Cole took a deep breath and sighed. "There have been a series of arson fires in the city, all Southeast Asian businesses. My office got some oddball messages. I ignored them. I've been so focused on the Jesse Monday thing, I just didn't want to be bothered. Bad call on my part, I guess. Yesterday on my way to lunch I was accosted by a guy with a gun, or so I thought. Turns out it was a piece of pipe he stuck in my back. The guy demanded I write the story of his great mission to clean up the city of immigrants. Of course, I had to pop off something, so he knocked me on the head. As I'm sure Dr. Ben must have told you, I popped off three times. The last time knocked me cold and I woke up zip-tied to a bus bench, being worked on by a paramedic."

"And he followed you to my house and tried to burn you up in it? My goodness Cole, why didn't you call the police when you were attacked?"

"I didn't have to, they were there when I woke up. In fact, the nice officer helped me across the street." Cole said in a mock child's voice.

"I'm trying to be serious here." Kelly scolded.

"I'm sorry. I was just so worried about feeding the fish that I..."

"Stop!" Kelly's voice cracked. "You scare me. You get clubbed unconscious and you don't think that is serious enough to get help?" Her eyes filled with tears. "Did you even bother to see a doctor?"

"No, I didn't. Listen, what were the chances the guy would follow me all the way to Sausalito?"

"100%."

"Good one. OK, I should have seen a doctor. But honestly, I wanted to..."

"Wanted to what? Change into your Superman tights? Honestly, Cole." Kelly looked down at the floor. "I need you."

"I will call Leonard Chin. I will write the piece the arsonist won't see coming and I will stick around to irritate you a while longer."

Kelly scowled and then broke into a smile. "What more can I ask?"

* * *

"Wakey, wakey." The voice of Charlie Baranski pierced the darkness.

"Leave me alone."

Don Wiltz was wrapped like a cocoon in a fleece blanket wedged between the back of the sofa and the wall. His lips were pressed hard against the fabric as he sucked in air through the acrylic filter of the blanket.

"I killed that newspaperman," Wiltz sobbed.

"Good."

Wiltz kicked his legs hard against the wall. "That was not war!"

"Collateral damage," Charlie said sarcastically. "I'm getting really sick of your sniveling and whining."

"Then leave me alone, damn you! I am through with you, and the fires."

"I'm not sure you know what you're asking, Donnie boy. If I go, so do you. We are one, you and I. Two minds, one body. To kill one kills both."

"I won't kill myself!"

"Then I guess you're stuck with me," Charlie chuckled. "Now, we have one last mission. Are you ready to put on your big boy pants and do your job, soldier?"

"One. One more? Swear?"

"Cross my heart and hope you die." Charlie laughed. "Come on, that was a good one."

"One more. I will do one more, then I am through. I never signed up to kill anyone."

"What do you think soldiers do? They kill as many of the enemy as they can and blow up, burn, and destroy as much of the other guy's stuff as they can. They don't quit until the enemy gives up. You did sign up."

One hand, and then the other, appeared from the tightly wound blanket. Wiltz pulled his head away from the fibrous mask and took in a deep breath. With his back against the wall, Wiltz used his knees and arms to push the sofa away from him. The blanket fell to the floor as he stood in the blackness of his living room.

A small orange light appeared in the corner of the room. As it grew, Wiltz saw a flame. The fire crawled up the wall. In front of him was the nail shop. The fire spread, and to his right, bright flames engulfed the pho restaurant. The room grew hotter and Wiltz folded his arms across the top of his head. As the flames moved across the ceiling, the image of the temple appeared to his left. He was surrounded by the blazing images of the infernos he created.

Up from the floor like an elaborate stage production came the houseboat in perfect miniature, and standing on top of it was Cole Sage! As Wiltz watched, Sage's arms spread and the flames climbed his body and melted him like a candle.

With arms outstretched and eyes tightly shut, Wiltz stumbled across the living room to the light switch. Making his way into the kitchen, he splashed his face in the kitchen sink. The clock on the microwave read seven-thirty. He must go to work.

Shortly after eight o'clock, Don Wiltz walked into the VA Hospital. His secretary stood as he approached her desk.

"Good morning," Terri offered.

"Good morning, Terri, nice to see you. Can I have a word?" Wiltz continued into his office.

"Of course," she said to his back.

Wiltz waited, holding the door. He softly closed it behind Terri. She took the chair in front of his desk. Wiltz stood.

"I have to apologize for my behavior of late. I have not been myself."

"Is there anything I can do?"

"No, I have just been struggling with the direction my life has taken, is taking, and I know I have treated you unfairly. I want to apologize for standing you up the other night. I, well, I..." Wiltz took a deep breath trying to gather his thoughts. "I cannot be involved in a relationship. You are a very kind and lovely woman. You deserve a lot more than I can give. Believe me, it..."

"I love you, Don," Terri blurted out, cutting him off midsentence.

"I believe I could love you too, Terri, but..."

"There are no buts. I have done everything I can to get you to acknowledge me. I've worked in this pointless job for over two years. I hate it. I'm tired of dealing with the sick people war has destroyed. I would've quit long ago except for you." Terri stood and moved to Wiltz's side of the desk. "I've waited for your attention, affection, a sign or something."

"I've been by myself for a very long time." Wiltz broke in. "There are reasons I'm alone."

"We could be happy, I know we could." Terri reached out and stroked Wiltz's cheek.

Wiltz stood, spun around and put his hands to his ears. Terri moved to where he stood. She slowly and tentatively reached out and put her arms around his waist.

"Please, Don, don't refuse me," she whispered, as her hands moved down and fumbled with his belt buckle. "Love me."

"Tell her you got your balls blown off!" Charlie laughed. "This is hysterical!"

Wiltz stiffened and pulled away. "I have nothing for you."

"Don't say that. You have everything I could want."

"No, I don't," Wiltz said forcefully. "This isn't working. I think you should go back to your desk."

Terri shoved Wiltz hard on the shoulders with both hands. "Other men have offered me attention. Other men think I am attractive, but I have waited for you. I have spoiled my chance with them. I have needs, too. I'm not getting any younger. I need someone. I chose you and you have thrown my affection back in my face! I don't understand what's going on, but I don't like it. You have led me on, and drawn me to you, and now you just say you have nothing for me!" Terri's voice seethed with the knowledge of her rejection.

"No balls, no balls, the Gooks blew off Donnie's balls!" Charlie sang mockingly. "The lady wants a lover, the lady wants a man, and Donnie can't find his man thing if he uses both hands." Charlie laughed hysterically at his dirty little ditty.

"Shut up!" Wiltz screamed at Charlie, but Terri was the only one there to hear.

"You bastard! You'll be sorry!" Terri left the office and slammed the door behind her.

The phone rang at Wiltz's desk. He spun and picked it up and threw it at the wall.

* * *

"Knock, knock," Hanna said, rapping the open door with her knuckles.

"Well, hello!" Cole said brightly. "You come to break me out of here?"

"I'm not sure about that, but I brought you this." Hanna held up Cole's laptop.

"A link to civilization! I have got to get out of here. I haven't seen a doctor since yesterday. I feel fine. I have stuff to do. How do I get these stupid things out of my arm?" Cole waved his arms, displaying his dangling IV tubes.

"Geez, what kind of drugs did they give you in here? Aggressive-een?"

"Too intense?" Cole grinned.

"A bit."

"So what have I missed?"

"Ruth is circulating a get-well card. They finally filled the snack machine in the break room. The men's room toilet overflowed and had to be closed. We got our staff 'Spring Fling' Tahoe Fun Bus flyer."

"Nurse! I've decided I want to die!" Cole called toward the door.

"The big news upstairs is holding the front page above the fold for your take on the arsonist and your attack."

"I gotta get out of here," Cole said, throwing his legs over the side of the bed.

"Whoa, big fella! That gives a whole new meaning to Southern Exposure!"

Cole grabbed at the back of his gaping gown and stood. "Very funny. Can you get a nurse or someone to get this thing out of my arm?"

"Too late," Hanna whispered.

"And what is it you're trying to do, Mr. Sage?" The scowling woman in the crisp white uniform was moving around the bed.

Hanna grimaced and moved back.

"I am checkin' out," Cole responded.

"Not without Doctor's say-so."

"Here's the deal. I don't like doctors, except my son-in-law, and sometimes he is iffy. I got a question for you—who's the patient here?"

"You are, of course."

"That makes me the customer. Right?"

"We like to think of you as a consumer."

"Who pays the bill for all this fine service I'm consuming?"

"You do."

"As the customer, or consumer, and the guy who is paying for all this, I'm done. I am exercising my right as a consumer to no longer use this service." Cole waved his arm at the nurse. "Now, can you get these out of my arm so I can get dressed?"

"This is not a good idea," the nurse said to Hanna.

"He's the boss. At least he's my boss, and I've learned his ideas are pretty much what happens." Hanna smiled and shrugged at the nurse.

Thirty minutes later, Cole climbed out of Hanna's VW Beetle and made his way into the *Chronicle* building.

"Hey, what are you doing here?" Cole said, approaching Leonard Chin who sat comfortably at Hanna's desk reading the newspaper.

"A little bird told me you were on your way here," Chin said, standing. "Is this dress-down day?"

"Kelly brought these to the hospital." Cole looked down at his Bay to Breakers t-shirt. "I was just going to call you."

"You know, Sage, sometimes I think there is something really wrong with you."

"How's that?"

"You are about three egg rolls short of a #9 lunch special."

"Did I just hear a joke, Lieutenant Chin?"

"I have been saving that one for just such an occasion." Chin grinned uncharacteristically. "I can't believe you didn't call me when you got knocked in the head by the guy lighting all these fires. What the hell were you thinking?" The humor was gone and Chin scowled at Cole.

"You're right. I was wrong."

"That's a start."

"I thought he was trying to scare me into writing 'his' story," Cole began. "We know how that turned out last time. I mean, who follows someone home and sets their house on fire? Scratch that. Dumb question."

"Do you have any idea who he is?"

"He made reference to Vietnam, but honestly, that means nothing."

"I don't know if you've heard but now he's torched the Vietnamese Buddhist Temple. Two monks sleeping upstairs are dead. So now it's murder."

"And he tried to incinerate me!" Cole responded.

"That doesn't count. Not my jurisdiction." Chin grinned again. "What do you remember? Voice? Did you see anything?"

"I didn't see a thing. He walked up behind me at the light, shoved what I thought was a gun in my back, and told me to cross the street. He sat me down on the bus bench, gave me a whack to each side of the head, and then boom, out go the lights. The officer at the scene took the pipe he hit me with. I doubt if it has prints."

"That's it?"

"'Fraid so."

"You know I don't like playing the Cop Card. This time I have no choice. If you hear from this guy again I have to know about it. You get it? I know you come from the Humphrey Bogart School of Tough Guy Reporters, but this time it came way too close to dead, Cole. No more funny business."

"Got it. By the way, anything new on Jesse Monday?"

"Risen savior scheme gone wrong is the general consensus." Chin shrugged.

Cole started to speak but burst into a deep, hacking cough.

"OK, if you're going to do the Doc Holiday to my Wyatt Earp, I'm out of here," Chin said, chuckling at his own witty remark.

Cole rubbed his eyes and smiled. "Way better than the egg rolls thing." "I'm back," Hanna said, sticking her head in the door.

"Snitch," Cole said.

"We prefer Confidential Informant." Chin stood and pointed his long index finger at Cole. "I meant what I said."

"I heard you loud and clear."

"Hearing's not doing."

"OK, you have my word."

"Better." Chin nodded and left Cole's office.

Hanna placed a small stack of newspapers on Cole's desk. "In case you want to see what you missed.

Cole flipped over the paper on the top of the stack, and scanned the headlines, and laid it aside. The next two he did the same. At the photo of Jesse Monday spread across the top of the front page, Cole froze. It wasn't the image of Jesse that caught his eye. The EMT standing in the ambulance door looked like a bystander, not an active participant in an emergency. In fact, there was no urgency in his demeanor.

It only took two rings for Randy Callen to pick up. "Basement subterfuge and computer tyranny."

"Just what I was looking for!"

"Cole, I was just thinking about you. Are you all right?" Randy's voice turned to heartfelt sincerity.

"I feel like I smoked a carton of Camels, but I'm coughing it out."

"I'm glad you're back. I've been doing some digging on your friends at Jesse Monday, Inc."

"Yeah?"

"It seems your friend Mr. Evans hasn't always had fleece as white as snow. It seems he was the fleecer."

"How's that?" Cole asked eagerly.

"Mr. Skeeter né Alan Lee Evans, did eight years in Folsom for mail fraud, running a Ponzi scheme, and get this, claiming it was a church fundraiser."

"This is a crazy idea, a long shot at best. I need you to find out everything you can about the two guys on the ambulance that went to pick up Jesse Monday."

"Full treatment?" Randy asked.

"Everything. Especially the guy in the photo we used. Who is he? I think I will pay him a visit."

"Are you up to that?" Randy's voice showed his surprise.

"I am not a desk jockey, contrary to the wishes of several women in my life. You get me the where, and I will worry about the how. Does that sound sick to you?"

"Depends on the definition of 'sick,' Are you looking for Webster's or Urban?"

"Everybody has their funny on today." Cole teased. "Get to work!"

"Yes, fearless leader!" Randy rang off.

"I love that kid!" Cole said to Hanna as she approached his door.

Hanna came in and gripped the back of the chair facing Cole's desk. She wasn't smiling, and her usually bubbly persona was replaced by a tense hesitant stance.

"It seems we need to do some serious reviewing of your job description, Ms. Day."

"Yes, sir." Hanna didn't look up. "I can explain."

"I have been here nearly a half-hour, and I have no mocha on my desk or any sign of it appearing in the near future."

"I'll go get it."

"Please do."

Cole chuckled to himself as she passed her desk. "Gotcha!"

A few minutes later Hanna reappeared, steaming cup in hand and as her old perky self.

"So, now you want to tell me about your visit with Skeeter Evans?"

"That was dirty, I came to confess."

"I needed you to relax. What did you find out?"

"You're not mad?" Hanna asked tentatively.

"I knew what I was getting when I hired you. You showed initiative, that's good. However, you're not a reporter and that creates a problem. Your friend Mr. Evans paid me a visit while I was in the hospital. Three a.m. to be precise. He wasn't pleasant. He sensed that you have an agenda. A good reporter never lets their personal feelings or beliefs get in the way of the facts."

"What did you tell him?"

"That I would get out of my bed and beat him up."

"Funny. I am sorry, but..."

Cole cut her off. "Sentences that start with *I'm sorry* should never have *but* as a conjunction."

"I am sorry. I did what I thought was best at the time. You couldn't go, so I did."

"Well, I did say I needed an assistant. You assisted, so case closed." Cole smiled. "In the future, the title is assistant, not reporter, clear?"

"Crystal." Hanna smiled sheepishly.

"So what'd you learn?"

"Two observations. First thing is that Skeeter never used the word dead when referring to Jesse. He said 'gone.' Second, that he is totally nuts. He's assumed the role of Messiah. He's not on a spiritual mission. He admits he's no preacher. In his own words, he is all about the power."

"There is something here. You have reinforced something that has been bugging me. Look at this." Cole turned the paper with Jesse's "death" and pointed at the EMT. "Look at this guy. What do you think he's thinking? Certainly not 'hurry up and let's get him to the hospital.'"

"He looks guilty," Hanna said flatly.

"Exactly. So, what has he got to feel guilty about? That's what we need to find out."

"Do we know who he is?"

"I've got Randy on that one."

"What do you want me to do?" Hanna's enthusiasm was checked by Cole's frown.

"Have you written up your interview?"

"Yes, done. I did it last night."

"Do you sleep?"

The phone on Cole's desk rang. "I bet that's Randy." Cole picked up. "Sage."

"Are you sitting down? Of course you are, you sit at a desk."

"Not always."

"Oh, I forgot you do the fire-proof sofa tester thing on your off hours."

"Funny boy. What have you got?"

"Ryan Marcus Crowder, the driver, twenty-three. 1421 South Peppermint Lane, San Leandro. Single, lives with his mother, Melody, and stepfather Curtis Seiford. Two older siblings live out of state. Pretty standard all-American kid, right? Here's the good part. He left for a backpacking adventure through Europe. When, you may ask? The day after Jesse was killed. Told everybody but his boss.

"Your guy in the picture? One, Tyler Bascom Linklater, twenty-six of 413 South West 28th Street, apartment C, in the city by the bay. He's suddenly paid off over nine thousand dollars in credit card debt and bought a brand new Yamaha R3 motorcycle. Oh yeah, and he took a couple of days off to go on a road trip. Both his boss and roommate confirm it. I'll send it all over in an email." Randy finished with a cheerful, "Whew!"

"Just what I needed. Thank you, sir," Cole offered.

"Invoice forthcoming. Later!"

Cole hung up the phone and took a long moment before speaking to Hanna. "In for a penny, in for a pound?"

"Meaning?" Hanna said, quizzically.

"You wanna drive?"

As the pair walked to Hanna's car, Cole coughed repeatedly as the cool air replaced the last remnants of smoke in his lungs.

"We look awful," Hanna said. "I figured I would go home and change before going in to work."

"I interviewed a multi-level insurance marketing guy years ago. He said if you're going to skin a skunk, dress for it." Cole smiled. "Linklater will never see us coming."

Driving across town, Cole looked out the window, occasionally commenting on the surroundings and genuinely enjoying the ride. "I never thought I would feel at home outside of Chicago. But I have truly fallen in love with this place. When I lived back east, I remembered my times as a kid going to concerts and a couple of anti-war marches. It wasn't until I moved here I realized how really small it is."

Hanna didn't reply and Cole fell back into silence. It only took fifteen minutes to get to 28th Street. Hanna pulled into a parking place right in front of the large sand-colored apartment building at 413.

"It was meant to be." Hanna smiled, turning off the engine.

"Listen, Watson, let me do the talking, All right?"

"Yes, sir."

The building was newly remodeled and was bright, clean, and modern. The door of the apartment they wanted announced itself with a shiny brass letter "C." Cole rapped the freshly painted door three times, and harder than Hanna thought necessary.

"Is that sixty seconds?" Cole asked.

"Probably."

Cole knocked two times and was about to knock again when they heard the deadbolt turn. The door opened and a sleepy-eyed young man in his early twenties stood rubbing his hands through his hair and gawking at his visitors.

"Yeah."

"Did we wake you?" Cole asked.

"Yeah. I pulled a night shift last night."

"Is Tyler around?"

"If he was, I wouldn't have had to answer the door, would I?"

"Know when he'll be back?"

"Nope. He bought a new bike and said he was going for a ride. That was three days ago. Haven't seen him since," the roommate explained.

"An R3, right? Nice bike. Do you ride?"

"Me? No, can't afford it. It's all I can do to pay the rent and eat." The young man smiled for the first time.

"I'm Cole Sage, by the way." Cole extended his hand to the young man.

"Efren."

"Sorry, this is Hanna." Cole offered. Hanna smiled. "Tell me something, do you have a cell number for Tyler? I really need to talk to him."

"Who are you again?"

"Cole Sage, I write for the *Chronicle*."

"Not a cop?" Efren asked, rubbing his eyes.

"No, why would you ask that?" Cole set the hook.

Efren cleared his throat. "Tyler is a good guy, a really good guy. I'm kind of worried. I mean, not worried exactly, but *something* happened a few days ago."

"Is he OK?" Cole injected.

"Yeah, nothing bad. The complete opposite actually. It was like he won the lottery or the keys to Disneyland or something. Then he bought that crazy motorcycle. Have you seen one of those things? Crazy fast."

"Did you ask him what happened?"

"Oh hell, yeah. I asked where he came up with the money to buy a motorcycle. He's like me—zee-row credit. Nobody's going to finance that thing. He said the money came from God! God? Since when does God hand out five grand for motorcycles?"

Cole looked at Hanna. "Let me ask you something. Are you an EMT, too? You said you worked all night."

"I'm a paramedic, actually. Tyler is the EMT, which makes his sudden riches even stranger, know what I mean? We're paid good, but San Francisco is expensive."

"I know what you mean. About that number," Cole pressed.

"If he's in trouble or done something crazy, you can help, right? Not just turn him over to the cops?"

"I have a feeling there is a very logical, unethical, but not totally illegal, reason for your friend's new-found funds."

The struggle of handing out Tyler's phone number showed on Efren's face.

"If we can talk to him, I think we can get this whole thing straightened out before the police get involved. If we've figured out something's up, they can't be far behind. Cops aren't all that smart, right?" Hanna smiled and winked at Efren.

"You got that right. I guess it can't hurt." Efren spoke directly to Hanna. "Ready?"

Hanna punched the numbers into her cell phone. Cole stepped back, giving Hanna space to finish the interview.

"Can I have your number, too? I'll let you know when we find something out if you want." Hanna offered.

"That would be great. Thank you."

"We appreciate your help, Efren. You'd probably like to get back to sleep, huh?"

"Yeah, I'm really dead. I hope you can help Tyler. He's a good guy." Efren closed the door.

"Cops aren't all that smart?" Cole jibbed, turning to Hanna.

"We're here first, aren't we?"

"There is that," Cole said, obviously impressed with his new partner.

As they got back in the car, Cole pondered what his next step was. Tyler Linklater could be anywhere.

"So, what are you waiting for?" Hanna closed her car door.

"What?"

"Aren't you going to call?"

"Actually, I was thinking about where he could be."

"Only one way to find out." Hanna wasn't going to let Cole off the hook.

"Are you hungry? It is lunch time." Cole teased.

"Call already!"

Hanna gave Cole the number and he called Tyler Linklater's phone. After several rings, a voice came on the line. "Hello?"

"Tyler?"

"Yeah," he said, hesitantly.

"How's the new bike?" Cole asked.

"Awesome. I'm totally loving it."

"Where are you?"

"Who is this?"

"Cole Sage, I was just talking to Efren. I told him I would give you a call. How you doin'?"

"Do I know you?"

"No, not yet. I write for the *Chronicle*," Cole said cheerfully.

There was a long pause. Cole held his breath. Tyler's next words were key to what he hoped to find out.

"Am I in trouble?"

"I hope not. Are you worried?"

"What was your name again?"

"Cole."

"I think I may have done something that, I don't know, something that might come back to bite me."

"Is there anything I can do to help? Would you like to talk?" Cole said, reassuringly.

"I probably need to. But what are you going to write? I mean, I promised to not tell, I mean, oh crap. I really need to tell someone but I am really torn."

"Where are you, Tyler?"

"Stinson Beach. Just pulled over to watch the waves."

"I love that place. How about I drive up and we have a chat? I can be there in an hour or less. Do you know the Lunch Box?"

"No," Tyler replied.

"It's a little place on Calle Del Mar. How about I buy lunch and we have a talk?"

"If I can find it."

"Ask anybody, it's easy. Look, it's a quarter to eleven. I'll see you there at noon. How's that?"

"How will I know you?"

"I'll be in a tan VW Beetle. Are we good?"

"Yeah, we're good. I'll see ya."

"See you soon." Cole smiled at Hanna. "Hungry?"

NINE

It was a glorious day in San Francisco. The sky was filled with rolling balls of white sourdough mounds of clouds. The brilliant turquoise blue that lay beyond made their canyons and majestic rolling forms seem to glow in the sunlight. A gusty breeze swept through the city like a giant series of inhales and exhales, cleansing the city of the tired air of the day before. It was a great day for a drive.

Hanna didn't so much drive as she attacked the streets of San Francisco. Cole tried to not seem effected by her downshifting, hard-braking, passing going downhill, and total disregard for stop signs as she crested hills. It was kind of stimulating to see someone, especially a woman, take such pure joy in the act of driving. He wouldn't have been surprised if she yelled, "Yeee Haw!" as she nearly went airborne, flying through an intersection and descending a steep hill.

All the fun stopped as she turned onto Van Ness. Heavy traffic and frequent stop signals brought her Volkswagen version of *Bullitt* to an end. Cole admitted he felt a thrill just being along for the ride. Besides, she was a lot cuter than Steve McQueen!

"So, what have you got to listen to?" Cole inquired.

Hanna reached over and popped open the glove box, exposing a zipper binder of CDs. "Take your pick."

Cole unzipped the folder and began flipping through titles. The Eagles, Pere Ubu, Mandy Patinkin, Allison Krause, Ferdinando Carulli's "Arrangement for Guitar and Piano of Beethoven's Variations in F, Op. 169," and "The Best of Dan Hicks and His Hot Licks." Cole stopped and looked at Hanna. There was more to this woman than he'd imagined. He flipped through several more titles before deciding on a homemade, hand-printed disc that read "Grateful Dead – Radio City - 10/31/1980."

"Here we go," Cole said, slipping the disc into the player.

The crowd's roar covered the first few notes of *Heaven Help the Fool*, but Cole smiled as Bob Weir began to sing.

"Tell me something," Cole began again. "Jerry or Bob?"

"Jerry."

"Good."

"Now you tell me something."

"All right," Cole replied, figuring he would be given a choice between Keith and Donna Godchaux, love 'em or hate 'em, or Pigpen or Brent Mydland? He was not prepared for what followed.

"Are you happy?"

Cole was caught totally off guard. "Happy?" he repeated.

"Yeah. Happy."

"Happy or content? There is a difference, you know. For years I have kept that old green Japanese paperweight on my desk." Cole stated.

"That thing that looks like a coin?"

"Yeah, I got it years and years ago in Kyoto. I asked a Japanese friend at the time to write down the meaning. He did, but we got distracted and didn't talk about it. All the slip of paper said was "Learn to be Content." I have always wondered, does it mean to learn to be content in your surroundings, or does learning make you content? Two entirely different things. Kind of like being happy. I'm happy to have a job, I'm happy where I live, and I'm happy to have Kelly in my life. But do I go around with a Cheshire Cat grin on my face? No."

"So, are you content?" Hanna asked, still trying to process the difference.

"No. Never have been. Never will be."

"Why not?"

For a long moment, Cole reflected on where this was going. He decided before waxing eloquent on his philosophy, he'd better get to the root of the inquiry.

He thought of the story he once heard of the little boy who asked his father where babies came from. The father, in sheer terror, began down the road of mommy and daddy love each other, and men and women are made different, and a painfully embarrassing explanation of things.

After several minutes of biological reproductive education, he inquired of the boy, "Does that help?"

"Not really," the boy said, a bit bemused. "I meant the big building downtown where Timmy was born."

Cole looked across at Hanna. "Are you happy?"

"Go on about the content part. Why aren't you content? Don't get off topic."

"I have always struggled with contentment. In church, I always wriggle in my seat when they read the twenty-third Psalm. "The Lord is my shepherd; I shall not want." I mean I believe it, and I try to live it, but that is one I really have a hard time with."

"Why aren't you content?" Hanna was genuinely interested.

"I'm not sure. Maybe it was being an only child. But as long as I can remember, nothing was quite good enough. God knows, I'm not a perfectionist, but there always seemed like there was more, something else, a different answer.

"I remember seeing the *Wizard of Oz* as a little kid and crying because I didn't want Dorothy to go back to black and white. My work is the same way. I write a column or a feature, and it never feels quite finished. Worse yet, it never feels like it will make a difference." Cole shrugged.

"What about your life away from work?" Hanna pressed.

"Even worse," Cole laughed. "I can't be satisfied. I literally can't get no satisfaction. I want to be a better dad, a better grandfather, a better..." Cole paused.

"Better what?" Hanna said, feeling a bit uncomfortable with the blank needing to be filled in.

"I feel silly saying boyfriend. Or *whatever* I am to Kelly."

"Boyfriend is fine, but are you satisfied with your relationship?"

"Nope." Cole reached over and turned down the music. "I feel like I'm letting her down, not taking our relationship further. To tell you the truth, I am terrified at the cliff that's in front of me."

"How do you mean?"

"I've been alone so long. It is that whole contentment thing. I longed for Erin's mother for nearly my whole life. I waited, hoped, dreamed, and then finally gave up. We could have spent our entire lives together. Instead, my discontent drove me to take a job that ended it all. Then my inability to be content drove me further away. When I looked up, I realized I'd lost the only thing that could have ever made me content."

Cole cleared his throat. He wasn't sure how he let so much out. No turning back now, he thought.

"I think Kelly may just be where I finally find contentment. Silly talk for a guy way closer to retirement than from it." Cole paused. "How about you? Are you happy?" Cole knew he would not speak until she responded.

Hanna reached over and turned the music back up. "I like this one." *It Must Have Been the Roses* filled the car. Cole didn't move.

"I am very lonely," Hanna said after a minute. "I have spent way too long alone, too. I'm happy, too.

I can't wait to go to work each day. Truly. It is the most fulfilling thing I have ever done. We never get to talk, I mean, really talk. I just want to say thank you for taking a chance on me. I know I screw up a lot and have oceans of stuff to learn, but I'm so grateful."

"That's wonderful. You have come a long way. I probably don't say it enough, if ever, but you are exactly what I need at that desk."

"Enough, this is getting icky. I want to know more about the content part. You know, I'm not into religion or spiritual stuff. I tried Transcendental Meditation and Kabbalah. And nothin.' You know what I mean?" Hanna flicked on her turn signal and moved to the center lane as they pulled onto the Golden Gate Bridge. "I know you're into your faith, but it's different. You don't try to preach to me or convert me. I appreciate you respecting my beliefs or lack of them." Hanna laughed.

"I didn't always have a strong belief in anything. I mean, I believed in God. But frankly, it didn't matter. Seeing Ellie, Erin's mom, again changed a lot of things. It was then I reevaluated what my core beliefs were, my world view, and I realized that if she believed that God was that real, then I must explore it, too. So my faith is very important to me. I am a work in progress and I will do and say things that won't be real Christian on occasion, probably too often, but I'm at fault, not God.

"The contentment thing is a constant struggle. I feel sometimes like I have been given so much and it still isn't enough. I feel so guilty for being such an in-

183

grate. But there is so much I want to do still—places to go, a book to write, things I want to share with my granddaughter. I want to sit for days and just look at Kelly's smile and listen to her talk. I can't do those things. There's work, bills to pay, promises to keep. And The Fight, it's always The Fight; truth, justice, and the American way! You know? Right the wrongs of the world, one word, in a newspaper, at a time." Cole gave her a melancholy smile.

"So how do I fix that in my life? I want to do what you do. I can't go back to school. I probably would do well if I did. I see the fat-ass secretaries around me and I think I can't end up like that. You know? I want to do things, too. Meeting Skeeter the other day was a rush like I have never felt in my life. My god, what if I could do that all the time! Do you ever get used to it? I loved it."

"That's the reason I can't give it up. But you can still do whatever you want."

"Not really. I squandered my past. I coulda, shoulda, woulda done a lot of things. I sat, stewed, and soured." Hanna sighed.

"Do you realize you're telling the story of over twenty-five years of my life? It took losing the person I loved most in the world to bring me to a place where I could see. We couldn't have had this conversation five years ago. We would have jumped off this bridge, hand-in-hand!" Cole laughed. "Not literally. But I reached a very sad, dark, miserable place. Watching Ellie die with such dignity, peace and grace made me realize what a gift life is."

"But how?"

"There is clarity when one grows more distant from their past. The older I get, the more I realize most of the things I love now, I could have begun long ago. I choose to press on through what I don't like, and toward the things I do."

They both sat listening to music and reflecting. Cole found his words were directed at himself as much as Hanna. There were changes he still needed to make. This time he was in charge, they were his changes, his way, and in his time.

"I'm willing to learn and do and help in any way I can. I know I said that in my interview, but those words have a different meaning now. You said I was exactly what you needed at my desk. Did you mean it, or were you just being nice?" Hanna pressed.

"I'm not that nice."

"I guess what I'm trying to say is thank you. We are kind of alike, and I think I have begun turning that corner since I've worked for you."

"With me?" Cole glanced at Hanna as a tear rolled down her cheek.

"Pigpen or Keith Godchaux?" She asked, softly.

"Donna." Cole chuckled. "Brent Mydland was the best singer."

This time Cole turned the music up, just in time for the opening chords of *Bird Song*.

Calle Del Mar is a pretty little street that leads to a nice park. It took some brain work on Cole's part to remember exactly how to get there. Hanna relied on her in-dash GPS. She humored Cole and let him think he was leading the way.

The Lunch Box is at the end of a tiny strip of shops that run at a ninety-degree angle with the street. As they pulled into the parking lot, Cole pointed out a young man sitting beneath an umbrella next to the Lunch Box sign.

"Bet that's him."

As they got out of the car, the young man stood.

"Mr. Cole?"

"Sage actually, but please call me Cole."

Tyler Linklater took Cole's outstretched hand. "Who's this?" Tyler didn't seem happy with the extra company.

"My chauffeur," Cole quipped.

"Hi, I'm Hanna, his administrative assistant. Are you hungry?"

"I really am."

"How about we grab something and eat out here?" Hanna smiled as she took control of the conversation.

A few minutes later the trio sat under a large faded red umbrella. Cole took it nice and slow. "Nice bike."

"Hella fast, too." Tyler beamed.

"How's the pulled pork?"

"Great." Tyler turned to Hanna, "What'd you get?"

"Tuna melt."

Cole took a big bite of his salmon po' boy and watched Hanna and the young man chat. They seemed to have made a connection and Cole wasn't going to rock the boat. He studied Hanna. There was a lot more to her than he imagined. She was warming the kid up like a pro, small talk, no leading questions, EMT stuff, lights, and sirens, was the training difficult. She was as far from Jesse Monday as a person could get.

Every time she took a bite or a sip of soda, Tyler would glance at Cole and smile.

"How long have you been a newspaper guy?" he finally asked Cole.

"Just over thirty-five years. I'm one of the old farts at the paper."

"You like it?"

Must be the day for it, Cole thought. "Yeah, love it. How about you, how long have you been an EMT?"

"About three years. It's pretty cool but I don't want to do it much longer."

"Really, what do want to do?" Hanna asked.

"I want to be a cop. That's kind of why I wanted to talk to you," Tyler said, looking Cole straight in the eyes.

There it was. People needed a reason to tell their story. Pride, guilt, remorse or fear. Tyler Linklater was scared.

"Why's that?" Hanna continued.

"Is this on the record?"

"You've been watching TV!" Hanna giggled. "No, it's not on the record. We'll tell you when to worry. I'm kidding. Please go on."

"I don't want something like this screwing up my chances to be in law enforcement, you know?" Tyler picked up a morsel of cabbage slaw from his sandwich wrapper. "I think I made a really bad choice."

The three sat quietly eating their lunch for several minutes.

"So where did you grow up?" Hanna broke the silence.

"Cupertino. Tino Pioneers baseball, and bag boy at Stevens Creek Market. I miss it sometimes."

"It's not far away," Hanna offered.

"Nothing to go back to now. My mom died three years ago, so you know, lots of memories. You kind of remind me of her in a lot of ways. Mostly your eyes. You have kind eyes."

"That's very nice. You must miss her a lot."

"A lot." Tyler nodded.

"How about your dad?" Cole asked.

"He left when I was three. We never heard from him again," Tyler replied.

"Tell me something, Tyler. What did you mean when you said you made a bad choice?"

Tyler looked at Hanna and then said, "The shooting. It was fake. The whole thing. That preacher. He's not dead."

"What do you mean?" Hanna was not prepared for the response she got.

"You're telling us that Jesse Monday is alive and well?"

"Yes, sir. I talked to him. He wasn't shot or anything. It was all faked. One big punk job on the world."

"Tell us about what happened. From the beginning." Hanna said reassuringly. "It is really important, Tyler."

"I swear to god, you are my mom." Tyler laughed. "She used to say that to me all the time. Maybe you should adopt me! You're really good at the mom thing."

"You're sweet. Please, what happened?" Hanna said, fighting back a lump in her throat.

"My partner Ryan and I were taking our break. There's a wide paved area that goes into the little park at Ashby and Fell. It's easy to get in and out of. Anyway, this guy walks up to the driver side window.

"The guy asks if we always park there. Ryan's kind of a smartass sometimes and he said, 'What's it to you.'

"'Maybe I'm talking to the wrong guys,' the guy says and starts to walk off.

"'About what?' Ryan called after him.

"I wish he would have kept his mouth shut." Tyler looked down and picked at his sandwich wrapper. "So, the guy turns around and comes back to the window. "Money," he says.

"'For what?' Ryan asked.

"'I need a little favor.'

"'We don't do drugs. Take, sell, hold, nothin,' Ryan replied.

"'Good,' he said. 'That's good. I just want you to do your job. Fifteen, twenty minutes tops. Then we forget we ever met.'

"I told Ryan I didn't like the guy, and that we should go. He wouldn't leave."

"'So what's in it for us?' Ryan asked sarcastically.

"Fifteen a piece.'"

"'Get lost,' Ryan said and started to roll up his window.

"'Grand," the guy said.

"'Fifteen thousand dollars? To do what exactly?'

"'It's simple, really. There's going to be a shooting.'

"'I'm out,' Ryan said.

"'It's fake. Staged. We need someone to disappear. The best way is if he's dead. He will appear to be shot. You guys will take the call, put him in the back, drive him to the hospital. Our people will take it from there.'

"How many laws is that breaking?" I asked him.

"'None. What I will insist on is that you turn off your radios during that time. You are off the clock, so to speak. Any problem with that? Nope," Ryan said. He was really excited.

"I really needed to ask some questions, like, how do we know the guy isn't really shot? Who is he? How do we get paid? Who the hell are you? You know? This is really weird. I swear, all I wanted to do is run. I do watch a lot of TV and this is the kind of shit that gets people killed." Tyler was getting agitated reliving the memory.

"So why'd you do it?" Hanna asked.

"Ryan. He convinced me we could do it in a heartbeat. So I asked my questions, got my answers, and agreed to go along with it."

"Who was the guy?" Cole asked.

"Skeeter something. Weird name, huh?"

"Yeah," Cole agreed.

"How did he find you?" Hanna asked.

"He said he'd been watching us. Saw we came there every day. He was staying across the street or something. I don't really remember."

"So how did you get paid?"

"He told us that he would call Ryan's cell phone in an hour. We would go to the Starbucks on Fulton. No more than three minutes, if that, from where we were. He would be there, flag us down, we would pick up the guy and go. He handed Ryan two envelopes. There was five grand in them. He said he would throw a backpack in with the guy we put in the ambulance. The rest would be in there. Crazy, huh?"

"Just like on TV," Cole said.

"This is the part that I'm worried about, though," Tyler began. "Ryan made a smart remark about taking off with the money. This Skeeter guy says, he found us once, he would find us again." Tyler shook his head. "He said if we told anyone, we would be real sorry. It was really scary the way he said it. Kind of like dead sorry, you know?"

"Is that why Ryan took off?" Cole asked.

"How'd you know that?"

"How'd we find you?" Cole said flatly.

Tyler shifted on the bench. Hanna looked at Cole and wadded up her sandwich wrapper. Cole chomped ice and watched a couple getting out of an Audi with a big, ugly dog.

"Why do people take big, nasty, slobbery things like that in a car with them?" Cole sneered.

"Love," Tyler said brightly. "You ever had a dog?"

"When I was a kid."

"Good times, right?"

"So what happened when you got to the hospital?" Cole said, getting back on track.

"Half a mile before we get there, a guy flagged us down and got in my side of the ambulance. I was in the back. He crawled into the back, gave, what did you say his name was, Jesse?"

"Yes."

"He gives Jesse a jacket, baseball cap and a sort of duffle bag, a suitcase kind of thing. Jesse goes up front. The guy gets on the gurney, we drive about a hundred yards and there's a cab. Jesse jumps out, gets in the cab and they're off." Tyler paused for a moment. "Here's the funny part. We went back into Emergency and there are two guys in scrubs waiting at the sliders. I open the back, and they rush up and pull out the gurney. That's my job. Hospital people never do it. Then, one of the guys winks at me and grins. They're Skeeter's guys! I watched them roll the "not Jesse" into the sliding doors. They turn left! Emergency is to the right. Nobody saw a thing!" Tyler was more animated than in the entire conversation. "I must admit, it was pretty slick."

"Just like on TV." Cole frowned and took a drink of his soda.

"Then what did you do?"

"Turned the radios back on. It was only sixteen minutes. Nobody even noticed. We drove back to the park. We opened the backpack, and sure enough, there was twenty thousand dollars. I wouldn't have cared if it wasn't there, you know, I mean I already got five thousand for doin' nothin'." Tyler laughed. "I know somehow it's wrong but, damn, that is a lot of money."

"So then?" Cole chimed in.

"We drove around and I realized we left the gurney at St. Mary's, so we drove over and found it right by the doors."

"What about the mortuary?" Hanna asked, more thinking out loud than a question for Tyler.

"I don't know. I guess Skeeter had that covered, too."

"You throw enough money around and you can get anything done. Right, Sport?"

"I guess so," Tyler replied.

"We appreciate you talking to us, Tyler. I think that there is a lot more to this story. Your friend Skeeter has some answering to do."

"Don't tell him you talked to me!"

"No, no, that won't be necessary," Hanna said calmly.

"The guy I want to talk to is Jesse Monday. You have been a great help, young man." Cole patted Tyler on the shoulder. "Let me tell you something. If I was your age, had been in your place, I would have probably done the same thing. Except I would have bought a Porsche. Money went a lot further back then!" Cole stood and said to Hanna, "Ready to go?"

"I've enjoyed chatting with you, Tyler." Hanna stood and offered him her hand.

"I feel like I had lunch with my mom. It really felt good. God bless you, it really meant a lot to me." To Hanna's amazement, Tyler jumped to his feet and gave her a hug.

As Hanna walked past Tyler's motorcycle, she turned and said, "You be careful on that thing!"

"Yes, mom!" Tyler called back.

"Mom? Really?" Cole teased.

* * *

As Cole and Hanna drove back toward the city, windows rolled down, and *Me and My Uncle* blasting from the stereo, Jesse Monday approached the front door of Miki and Mini Morgan.

Jesse stood for a long moment. He could hear voices through the door. He knew what he must do, what he would face, but it had to be done. He took a deep breath, breathed a prayer and gave the door three hard, hearty knocks.

The door opened and Miki Morgan gasped. "Jesse, is it you?"

"It's me."

The tiny woman threw her arms around his waist and wept. Moments later, Mini came to the door.

"Everyone, look! It is our Jesse! He is risen! I knew they all lied!"

As Jesse moved into the hallway and toward the living room, he saw familiar faces, some in tears, smiles and welcomes, some angry and silent.

"Hello, everyone," Jesse said, as he moved around the room, giving and receiving hugs and cold stiff handshakes.

Skeeter entered the room from the kitchen. He wore a smile as fake as Jesse's death. While the uninformed followers in the room basked in the light of their returning messiah, Skeeter saw betrayal and the breaking of covenants and agreements.

"Hello, Jesse," Skeeter said coldly.

The room grew quiet. The air fairly crackled with the intensity of the meeting. Miki and Mini sat pressed together in the corner of the couch, and several of the men stood in the doorways and along walls as if preparing for an earthquake. A soul-deep revelation flooded the room. Several people stood praying, tears running down their faces. An ominous presence was doing battle with the essence of goodness and light.

"Hello, old friend." Jesse offered without inflection.

"What are you doing here?"

Miki and Mini hugged each other, breathlessly staring at the two men.

"I knew the faithful would be gathered here and I thought I might have a word, before."

"Before what?" Skeeter said harshly.

"Oh, you are so transparent." Jesse smiled, nodded his head and laughed quietly.

"Listen, everyone," Jesse began.

"No, you listen! I will not have you come here and confuse those so young in the faith." Skeeter fired back.

"Faith? I believe faith is the substance of things hoped for, the evidence of things not seen. Isn't that right? These people hope for a better life, a life eternal, and a life lived abundantly. They certainly must have a lot of faith because, frankly Skeeter, we have shown little of late that they should have any faith in. You might say, 'the evidence of things unseen,' in this case is perhaps better unseen." Jesse spoke with a kind tone, and with the certainty of someone who believed every word he said.

Skeeter stood, arms crossed, and glaring defiantly at Jesse.

"Dear ones, listen to me. I have sinned and sinned mightily. Not only against the Almighty but you, the ones who loved and trusted me to show you the truth. I am going to tell you 'the Truth,' a truth I seemed to have lost sight of. My heart was turned by flattery.

"The great King David knew this kind of flattery. He told us long ago, 'Not a word from their mouth can be trusted; their heart is filled with malice. Their throat is an open grave; with their tongues, they tell lies.' He was speaking of the people around him who had motives that were less than pure.

"So I tell you this, leave here, leave this so-called ministry and take the light I have shown you and let it guide you to the true worship of the only true God. Find a church where the real truth is preached. Short of that, read your Bible. Start with St. John.

"I am through. I have taken my gift and squandered it. I have misled and betrayed your trust. I am right with my God now, but that doesn't undo the harm I have done. If you truly believe, go out and help heal what I have done. I love you all, but I am not worthy of your company. Perhaps someday we will meet again."

"What of your resurrection?" Miki asked.

"Oh, my sweet Miki. I was not dead. It was a treacherous fraud that, thank God, I came to my senses soon enough to abandon. Besides, you don't need me to show you the way. Pray to the Father and he will show what you need. I think in your heart of hearts you know that already."

"He has admitted it! He is a fraud!" Skeeter cried out. "He is a deceiver, stay with me. We can show the world the way. I can lead you. You don't need to give up. I have seen the angel of light and he has shown me our path. Trust me, I have been given the power over heaven and earth. I was not ready to come into my ministry, but he has torn away the curtain and I am come into my glory."

"You all know what you must do. Go home, find a place of prayer. I love you. I will pray for you, but I must go." Jesse turned and started for the door.

"Yes, go! You have trampled these hearts into the dirt. I will heal them. You are nothing. I will show them the way! We don't need you! I made you what you are. Without me, you are nothing, nothing!"

As Skeeter screamed at Jesse's back, one by one, the men and women in the room began to leave. None looked back at Skeeter.

"Skeeter, I think you should leave." Mini stood from the couch and faced the red-faced man who screamed toward the door.

"What? You too? I don't need you, either."

"You need more than us, Skeeter." Miki now stood by her sister.

"Why don't you two freaks call Mothra? Maybe he can save you from me!"

"You are an evil man. You are a hurtful man. You are the one Jesse was talking about. I want you to leave and not come back," Miki said, beginning to cry.

"I'll get my stuff." Skeeter turned and left the room. As he passed two men standing near the kitchen, he said, "Well, where do you stand?"

"There is something around you I like," said one man. "You seem to be in touch with some kind of power I want more of."

"Good, I'll need a ride."

The bigger of the two men shrugged. "I guess that means get the car."

Outside, a small group stood at the end of the drive, crying, hugging, and praying. They felt someone walk up to them. It was Jesse.

"Can someone loan me fifty cents? I need to make a phone call."

TEN

"So what now?" Hanna asked as they exited the elevator and headed for Cole's office.

"Write up everything you remember, inflections, expressions, body language, any and everything."

"What about quotes?"

"Did you record it? Take notes?"

"Well, no."

"If you're going to quote someone you better have a record. From the time we sat down until this minute," Cole looked at his watch. "Little over two hours. Nobody's memory is good enough to get it all word for word."

"Why didn't you say something?" Hanna pleaded.

"Aren't you the one who told Tyler it was off the record?"

"Well, yeah, but..."

"There you are, kiddo, Sage's Journalism Seminar 101. Always take notes, never promise off the record, and remember the five Ws and the H. Welcome to higher education."

"What Ws?" Hanna queried.

"That's one of them." Cole chuckled as they reached Hanna's desk. "You'll figure it out."

It only took a moment for Cole to hit the speed dial #1 after he sat down. "Lieutenant, I hope you're not driving."

"Cole, what's going on?"

"The Jesse Monday murder. Call off the dogs. There was no murder. No bullets either, for that matter. It was staged, faked, a hoax. Jesse Monday is alive as you and me. Well, at least you."

"What? Says who?"

"How about an anonymous source in the ambulance."

"I'm listening."

"With the help of my crackerjack staff, I located a firsthand witness. He states that the drivers of the ambulance were given fifteen grand apiece to drive, act the part, and deliver the old switch-a-roo. Alive and well, the real Jesse hopped in a cab, a replacement rode to the hospital to be seen by, who knows who, then delivered to a phony mortuary driver."

"I need to talk to this witness," Chin pressed.

"That will be tough. Seems I lost his name and contact info. Threw it away accidentally with my lunch trash."

"Bullshit!" Chin shouted.

"Nope, I had a salmon po' boy."

"So what am I supposed to do with this nameless, unconfirmable piece of worthless information?" Chin's anger was growing by the second.

"Hold on, hold on. I have the name of the mastermind of this little charade."

"Yeah?"

"Skeeter Evans. Monday's second-in-command, and instigator of the whole operation."

"Why didn't you say that in the first place?"

"Did anyone ever tell you how cute you are when you're angry?" Cole razzed.

"No, they certainly haven't."

"That's because you're not. Geez, Leonard, you really do need to lighten up."

"What do you suppose the point was?"

"Easter is coming."

"And?" Chin asked.

"When better to have a new messiah resurrect?"

"You're kidding. That's crazy. But the three days have come and gone."

"Therein, my friend, lies the real mystery. What happened? Where's Jesse?" Cole pondered.

"And I thought you were calling with something on the guy that knocked you in the head."

"To tell you the truth, I haven't given it a thought. This Jesse thing seems to have taken on a life of its own. I have one of my guys doing research on him, though. If anything turns up I'll give you a call," Cole finished.

"I'll go pay our Mr. Evans a visit, and see what I can shake up. Problem is, if the call didn't go out as a 911, there is no false report violation. The guys on the ambulance gave somebody a hell of an expensive taxi ride. Staging a "performance art piece" on the streets of San Francisco does require a permit, but who really cares? I guess the only thing that remains is where Mr.

Monday is?" Chin paused. "I'll let you know what turns up."

"Same here."

Over the course of the next hour, Cole wrote and deleted two drafts of the Jesse Monday story. In one, he showed too much distance. It had no feeling, just a list of facts, a straight news piece if you will. The other showed his contempt for the handlers of people who began on a legitimate path, only to have their heads filled with an overinflated image of something that wasn't true.

It is nothing new, from Elvis to Michael Jackson, with stops every hundred feet for politicians, actors, athletes, porn stars and the talking heads of TV and radio. Very few are told they are God's other son, but "all is vanity." If you are told of your beauty, intelligence, wonder, power, and majesty often enough, you're going to believe it.

Cole knew there was a third option. The problem was he didn't have anything from inside of Jesse's camp. Time was running out. His stint in the hospital bought him time, but Chuck Waddell wouldn't wait much longer. Not just for the column, but for his answer to Chris Ramos' eternal destiny. Cole could feel the tension building within himself.

The phone on Cole's desk rang, bringing him from his multiple thoughts.

"Yep."

"There is a man on the line who says he's at a pay phone and only has a few minutes. He claims he has answers to the Jesse Monday shooting."

"Seems to be our day for it. Put him through." Cole sat a little straighter in his chair and felt around his desk for a pen. "Sage."

Hanna strained to hear the one-sided conversation.

"Are you OK?" Cole said with concern. There was silence, then, "Time and place, I'm there," Cole replied.

Hanna strained so hard to hear her chair scooted towards Cole's door without her realizing. She quickly scrambled back as she heard Cole say, "Stay put. I'll be there in fifteen minutes."

The sound of Cole's chair hitting the credenza meant he was on his way out.

"Hey, lead-foot, you want to drive me to Pier 39? Fast?"

"You pay the ticket?" Hanna called back, already standing, purse in hand.

"And gas," Cole said, moving past her desk and toward the elevator.

To Cole's surprise, Hanna turned on Fifth Street, not Mission. She flew up Fifth and barely slowed when she took the turn onto Eddy. Cole found himself grasping the door handle, and could have sworn she made the turn onto Jones Street on two wheels.

Stop signs and signals were mere suggestions as Hanna took her foot from the accelerator just long enough to assure there was no cross traffic, or at least not within fifty yards. She finally was forced to come to a stop at Chestnut and Columbus.

"Better not press our luck," she said, watching the heavy cross traffic.

Powell was a mess and she made a quick turn onto Bay Street in front of a Muni Bus and cut across to Stockton. The turn onto North Point moments later made Cole cling to his door to keep from leaning hard on Hanna.

"Almost there," Hanna said, down-shifting to make the turn onto Grant. "Sure glad it's one-way our direction!" Hanna swerved to miss a car that was double-parked in front of an office. She slowed along the short stretch leading back to Beach Street. "Hold on!"

"I haven't stopped!" Cole returned.

With a quick glance right and left, Hanna shot across the four lanes of Beach and turned onto the frontage street in front of the Aquarium.

"I'll hop out at the overpass up there." Cole glanced at his watch. "Eight minutes! Sometime you gotta tell me where you learned to drive."

"I'll park—where are you going to be?"

"You can head on back to the office."

"But..."

"I think a cab sounds really relaxing," Cole panted. "Wish me luck!"

"With what?"

"That was Jesse Monday on the phone. I'm meeting him here." Cole was out of the car and the door closed before Hanna had a chance to respond.

The traffic at the Pier was fairly light. It wasn't exactly the high season for tourists, but Cole thought it was especially thin for such a nice day. As he started toward the Hard Rock, he could hear the strains of *El Condor Pasa* in the distance.

"You'd think they'd learn a different song," Cole said to no one. "I'd rather be a banana than the chimp," he sang to amuse himself as he walked. "I'd rather be the cereal than the bowl, yes I would."

As he approached the five men wearing colorful Peruvian ponchos and bowl haircuts, the music stopped. The men froze in place. A middle-aged woman in a purple and green hand-knit sweater stood, camera in hand, in front of the musicians, stunned by the reaction of the exotic flute blowers.

A man watching from the side walked up to the group and put a coin in the upturned bowler hat. The music instantly resumed. The woman, obviously not getting the drift of the situation, raised her camera. The music stopped.

Huffing and puffing, the woman turned, saying something about never liking that song anyway. As soon as she was ten paces away, the flutes began once more.

"Free market economy," Cole said to the man who left the tip as he passed him.

As he reached the Hard Rock Café, Cole stopped and gave the area a serious once-over. Jesse was nowhere to be seen.

"Great," Cole muttered.

The bright green bench looked inviting and he went and sat down where his vantage point covered most of the area and up the pier. It was frustrating to think he fell for another hoax. The tourists filed past in bunches and couples. As Cole watched, he realized that anyone who took a moment to look could spot those on the make, and especially the pickpockets. The excitement of being at Pier 39, the sea air, and sweeping seagulls everywhere are enough to distract anyone from the "accidental" brush of a passing figure. That is until they discover their wallet or cell phone is gone.

The man in a powder blue warm-up suit just passed him for the third time. *What's he up to?* Cole thought. The squealing of a pair of Japanese girls at the thrill of a seagull coming within inches of them redirected Cole's attention long enough for the man in the warm-up suit to take a seat next to him.

"Hello, Cole."

The voice was familiar, yet the man sitting next to him was a complete stranger. It took Cole a moment to process. The voice was Jesse Monday's. Gone was the beard and curly hair. His face and head were shaven smooth. The aviator shades covered the most distinguishing feature of Jesse's face. He could walk the streets unrecognized. The warm-up suit and jogging shoes made the polar opposite visuals complete.

"I didn't recognize you."

"Hide in plain sight, isn't that what they say?"

"That's what they say," Cole replied.

They sat for a minute watching a frustrated young couple with a stroller, arguing about which way to go.

"Kind of like life," Jesse finally said.

"It would be more like my life if they were pulling the stroller back and forth."

Both men gave a good-hearted chuckle.

"So, here we are." Cole brought the focus back to their meeting.

"I'm grateful."

"I intend to record our conversation. I don't want to be accused of misquoting or misrepresenting what you say. Is that going to be all right?" Cole reached in his pocket and took out a digital recorder.

"Fine."

"I guess the first thing is why'd you call me?"

"I've been sheltered from the press, the media, for a long time. You were the first journalist to be allowed access in I don't know how long. Yet you didn't ask any questions. You were just another guest at the table. That stuck with me. I couldn't seem to forget it." Jesse smiled and took off his sunglasses, "Sorry, better?"

"I always like to look a man, or woman, in the eyes when I talk to them. So yes, it helps, thank you."

"I called you because I want you, and in turn, the world, to know who I am. Without handlers."

"Skeeter, you mean?"

"Yeah. We came up together. I've known him a long, long time. But just like a beguiling angel of light, he was an imitation. And I was beguiled. You see, the bigger the crowds got, the bigger my head got, I guess. Skeeter saw that and took advantage of it. He can't be held solely responsible, because the sin of pride was great in me."

"Did you know he went to prison for running a religious scam?" Cole asked.

"Sure did. He seemed to repent. He walked the walk and talked the talk for quite a while before things began to change. In Jeremiah, it says, 'Can a leopard change its spots? Neither can those who are accustomed to doing evil.' I should have known better, I guess."

"None of us is perfect. I've had my head turned a couple of times in my life. Thought I was pretty hot stuff after receiving a couple of awards. I get it. But something or someone always knocked me back down to size. You have to admit this went a little overboard."

"Back when we started out, I started out, I was a kid with a love for Jesus and a gift of gab. I was the guest speaker who traveled around and spoke in churches. Skeeter got the idea to start preaching in parks. He knew how to rustle up a crowd. I thought he was just zealous."

"Sounds pretty naive to me," Cole interjected.

"I was naive. I came from a little dried-up speck of a town. My people weren't educated. They were hammer pounders. I thought my calling to preach gave me an excuse to blow off school, and I did. So I tend to take people on trust. That's not to say that we had no impact for God. We did. I'm just not too sure He is proud of how we achieved it."

"I first saw you about three years ago in Golden Gate Park on the meadow. There were some pretty strange things that happened that day."

"I was in full 'big head' mode at that point. I 'bit the apple' so to speak. I confess a lot of that was Skeeter's backstage showmanship. I figured as long as we drew crowds, and people heard the message, what did a little play-acting hurt?"

"It was fraud." Cole frowned.

"It was. No argument."

"Did you know that you have been under the scrutiny of the FBI and other government agencies?"

"Funny, isn't it? They would waste time and money followin' me around."

"Did you ever perform a miracle?"

"No. Did God do something for a true believer whose faith was in Him? Absolutely. I have no power. And to be real honest, after a while I think God took his hand off me."

"What are you saying?"

"I'm sayin' it was the Jesse and Skeeter Show. After a while," Jesse paused. "Did you ever hear the thing about puttin' a frog in cold water and turning the stove on? It'll swim around as the water gets warm, then hot until it cooks. You throw a frog into a boiling pot and it will hop right out. The water took so long to cook me I didn't even notice. Somewhere along the way, all eyes were on Jesse, and God got left by the side of the road. We got bolder and bolder in our claims, and folks came along for the ride. I was as bad, if not worse, than any of those hairspray clowns on the TV selling Jordan River water, or Miracle Handkerchiefs. The people who followed me would never sit for that, but they bought my line without a second thought. Different packaging, same snake oil."

"You sound bitter," Cole said.

"Bitter, no, I don't think that's it. What you hear is disgust with a heaping helping of anger."

"Anger?"

"At myself. I was despicable."

"So what changed?"

"Three little words. 'We did it.' They scared me to death," Jesse answered.

Cole sat quietly, waiting for Jesse to continue.

"So, that brings us up to the shooting?"

"Purdy much."

"Walk me through that."

"Well, it doesn't take a brain surgeon to figure out the next step for the Son of God is to rise from the dead!" Jesse laughed. "What blasphemy." Jesse's laughter was gone.

"Whose idea was it?"

"That one was all Skeeter."

"But you went along with it."

"I did. To my eternal shame. Look, here is the deal. I went along with his idea. It was stupid, vain, inspired by the devil. I get it. But the thing is, I ran. I'm still running. What do you think this get-up is all about?" Jesse ran his hand down his chest.

"Now what?"

"Just before I called you I went to Miki and Mini's house, where there was a gathering of the core faithful. Only Skeeter and a couple of hired hands were in on the shooting. So you can just imagine how happy he was to see me. Poor Miki thought I'd risen from the dead."

"What was the point of you going there?" Cole interrupted.

"Set the record straight and tell them to look to God and God only. Read their Bible. Find a good church, and don't be deceived by false prophets."

"How'd that go over?"

"Most everyone left. Skeeter went nuts, but his meal ticket just got cut off."

"Speaking of the need for funds, where's that leave you?"

"I borrowed a buck to call you."

"You serious?" Cole asked in disbelief.

"Matthew 6:25, brother! Matthew 6:25!"

"I'm a little rusty, remind me."

"Do not worry about your life, what you will eat or drink; or about your body, what you will wear. Isn't life more than food, and the body more than clothes? Look at the birds of the air; they do not sow or reap or store away in barns, and yet your heavenly Father feeds them. Aren't you just as valuable as they? Can you add a single hour to your life by worrying?" Jesse's voice suddenly turned into the street preacher again. "Hallelujah!"

"You can take the boy out of the pulpit..."

"I hope not," Jesse said meekly.

"Tell me, what do you think Skeeter will do now?"

"God help him, I don't know."

"One last thing, what was the 'Truth' you always spoke of? I never could quite figure it out." Cole smiled at Jesse.

"Chum in the water. Sumthin' to draw 'em in."

"So what is the 'Truth,' Jesse?"

"There is only one Son of God, and it ain't me." Jesse stood. "My turn to ask you somethin', Mr. Sage. You know in Bible times a sage was a man marked by great wisdom and calm judgment. I kinda get that from you."

"Ask away," Cole replied, having no idea where it was leading.

"What do I do now? I'm broke, and dead." Jesse chuckled.

Cole knew it was not an idle question or a cute way to end their talk. Jesse Monday was truly seeking his advice.

"My turn to preach." Cole was now standing, looking Jesse in the eyes. The guys in the Bible, from Moses to Jesus, would spend their 'forty days' in the desert. I think for your own mental and spiritual well-being, you need that desert time. I don't mean Death Valley, but you need to disappear. It's time for you to go...disappear for good."

Cole reached in his pocket and pulled out his money clip. He pulled the clip off the folded bunch of bills. "Here, one hundred, eighty-three dollars. Go as far as that will take you, and start over as someone else."

Jesse took the bills and gave Cole a bear hug. "God bless you, brother," Jesse whispered as he released Cole.

"Tell me something, Cole, what are you going to write?"

"An obituary," Cole said, smiling.

Jesse Monday put on his sunglasses and without a word, turned and walked away.

Cole walked over to a cart with a bright red and white umbrella. He was going to get an ice cream bar and sit and reflect on his encounter with Jesse. There was only one problem. He'd given Jesse all his cash and only had seventy-two cents in his pocket.

He wandered into the Hard Rock Café and sat at the end of the bar. He struck up a conversation with the bartender and bought a Coke with his credit card. He told the barman he let his cash get away from him and asked if he could use the phone to call the *Chronicle*.

"I can't let you do that," said the bartender.

"Here, buddy." A man down the bar slid his cell phone to Cole. "That story is too stupid not to be true."

Cole called Hanna and told her he would be waiting out front. No offer to pay tickets this time.

Twenty minutes later, Cole saw Hanna's beige Bug pull up. He didn't want to lie to her, but he didn't want to tell her Jesse was alive, either. His twenty minutes of clever preparation evaporated.

"Thanks." Cole paused for dramatic effect. "Again."

"So what did he say?"

"The guy that showed up was someone I'd never seen before. Kind of freaky, powder blue track-suit, and you'd swear he had alopecia." Cole buckled his seat belt.

"Yeah, what did you learn?"

"Skeeter's a rat. He's the mastermind behind the Jesse Movement. As you said, he's all about the power."

"Did Skeeter kill Jesse?"

"Nope. This guy saw the shooter. Wasn't Skeeter." So far, so true, Cole thought.

"Did he know what happened to Jesse's body?"

"Yes, well kind of. He said that Jesse was moved to a taxi. He didn't know who the mortuary guys were. So that's that."

"So now what?"

"I write the obituary and we let the police do their thing on the follow-up. The news guys can keep tabs on that. Then we shift gears to the arsonist."

"What about all my notes and stuff on Jesse?"

"Did anybody ever tell you, you ask questions like a reporter?"

"No, because I'm not," Hanna mocked.

"You've heard that one?"

"Yeah." Hanna downshifted and hit the gas.

Cole was greeted at his desk by a pink message slip with "Call Randy" scrawled across it diagonally.

"Hi, you just caught me. I was getting ready to call it a day. I think I found your guy," Randy said.

"And?" Cole said expectantly.

"Donald Peter Wiltz. Enlisted in September 1970. Assigned to the 10th Public Affairs Detachment, in Saigon, just like you thought. Served July '71 through Dec '73. Medical discharge. He was in the bombing of a Saigon nightclub. Get this, he was severely injured. He lost part of his upper thigh and genitals. Damn. If that doesn't make you squirm in your seat..."

"What makes you think he's our guy?"

"Your paths may have crossed again in Chicago. According to some medical records I accidentally stumbled onto, he not only took a while to heal, but he also spent almost two years in a Psych Hospital in Texas." Randy paused and Cole could hear his keyboard clicking. "Here we go, 'Upon release, he went to Central Illinois State College, earning a degree in Counseling. His Master's was in Psychology with a concentration in Counseling. Thesis title? Counseling Needs of Veterans with Post-war Trauma."

"He was kind of ahead of his time."

"His first job out of college was Jesse Brown VA Medical Center, Chicago, Illinois. Heard of it?"

"I know it well. They do great work," Cole replied.

"He spent almost twenty years there, then eight years ago came to San Francisco as Director of Outpatient Counseling Services. I bet a hundred bucks he's our guy."

"Randall, me lad, you are a wonder. How about you and I go have lunch at the goofy Fusion Mexi-Cali place you like so much?"

"Si, Senor dude!"

"Next Tuesday. Call and remind me," Cole said.

"That's three you owe me now."

"That's why I said to remind me. Now go home." Cole hung up and dialed Leonard Chin.

After six rings, Cole was given the message prompt. "Hey, it's Cole. I think I have something on the arsonist. Call me."

Hanna's head popped through the door. "Dare I ask how you're getting home?"

"I'm supposed to get a rental car tomorrow, today actually, but we kind of..."

"Five minutes?"

"Ten, and I fill your tank and buy dinner." Cole smiled hopefully.

"Serious, lunch and dinner?" Hanna said in amazement.

"Only if we hit an ATM first."

"Deal."

ELEVEN

"Good morning, Victoria. What are you doing here?" Don Wiltz smiled at the beautiful young Latina sitting at Terri's desk.

"Terri called in sick. They sent me over to help with scheduling."

"It's wonderful to see you. I hope you have a good day here. I'll try to go easy on you." Wiltz fairly gushed.

Truth be told, Don Wiltz would give everything he owned, then be willing to die, to spend just one hour being normal again and making love to this raven-haired beauty. He felt an embarrassed flush come over him. Did he say too much? Seem too eager? She was so lovely, though. Why couldn't he have a woman like her? He would take such good care of her. Not now, it was too late for him, but when he was young. He would have worshipped her, given her everything she could ever want. If only he was a whole man. He could have given her everything she ever wanted, except the one thing a beautiful young woman would need—a real man to fulfill her desires, her passion, and to someday give her children.

Wiltz left the door to his office open, so he could see Victoria. He loved the sound of her voice.

She had the faintest of accents and that was so very appealing to Wiltz. He felt normal. He didn't think of fires, he didn't heard the voice of Charlie Baranski. She was like a soothing angel come to free his mind and relax his soul. It was as if he found harmony between his body and spirit. There was no escaping it, he loved her. From the first time he saw her in the cafeteria, he had loved her, and it felt so good.

The morning went by far too quickly, Victoria setting appointments and introducing him to his clients for the day. He was loving his work. He listened and responded to the needs of the veterans who sat across his desk and felt their gratitude for his counseling. At eleven-forty-five, Wiltz got an idea, a fleeting thought, really.

He would ask Victoria out to lunch. He began to role-play different opening lines, and witty things he could say to charm her. It would be all right because he was so much older than her. *How old was she?* He wondered. *Twenty-five? Less, perhaps?* As the minutes ticked away to the lunch hour, Wiltz began to lose confidence. The palms of his hands were wet, his stomach churned, and he felt a tingling sensation of panic come over him.

At five to twelve, Don Wiltz stood up. He took a deep breath and started for the door.

"Donnie's got no pee-pee, Donnie's got no pee-pee." The sing-song taunt of Charlie Baranski filled the room.

"Stop it, stop it!" Wiltz whispered through gritted teeth.

"Go sit down, you old fool. She would laugh in your face. She can get a real man, a whole man, a man with..."

"Enough!" Wiltz growled and closed his office door.

The rest of the day was spent waiting for Victoria's gentle tap on his door and the next counseling session. He barely spoke to her the rest of the day, and at four-thirty she came in and said she was returning to her department to check messages, and catch any last-minute details for tomorrow.

Wiltz bid her good-bye. Defeated and inadequate, he watched her shapely form exit his office. He left his office at five, feeling deformed and alone.

The Banquet Mexican Style Frozen Dinner sitting on the table was only picked at. The clear plastic covering peeled back, but not removed, dripped with condensation. Wiltz just stared ahead. The image of Victoria kept running through his mind.

He drank mineral water and tried to watch television. Channel after channel he flicked up, then down, pausing only to catch glimpses of the local news, a game show, and an old Seinfeld episode. It seemed to Wiltz that all the other channels were just commercials. He turned the television off.

With his feet up, his shoes off, and the soft comfort of his recliner embracing his weary body, Donald Wiltz drifted into a dream of Victoria's soft breath on his neck, and her deep red lips softly whispering words of love in his idea of Spanish.

Victoria's soft skin, the smell of her hair, her soft sweet Mexican accent filled Wiltz with delight even if it were a dream. He watched her walk across the room to him, her smooth brown skin glowing in the candlelight.

"You are such a fine man," Victoria whispered.

"And I am a dead Vietnam veteran wanting you to wake up!" The sweet seductive tones of Victoria turned to the raspy anger of Charlie Baranski and jolted Wiltz from his dream.

"What a horny dog you are, Wiltz. Wake up and get ready, tonight is the night."

"This is it? The last mission?"

"If all goes well, we will examine that possibility."

"That's not good enough. I want your assurance that this is the last time," Wiltz demanded.

"OK, you have my dead man's hand pinky swear. Happy?"

Wiltz didn't respond, but he determined he was finished.

"Now can we continue?" Charlie began. "Have you done your reconnaissance of the target?"

"Three trips."

"How many stories?"

"Eight. One front entrance, two to the rear. Elevator from the lobby. Staircase from the original design. Looks to be from the thirties."

"Assault?"

"I will start on the fourth or fifth floor, to be determined by the number of hostile force I encounter."

"You are so good at this kind of work, I don't understand why you would ever want to quit," Charlie said in genuine confusion.

"Because it is wrong. We should never have started. People have died, Charlie. It isn't just buildings. People, living breathing people, burned to death."

"Gooks, nothing more, nothing less, the same Gooks who blew off your balls. I would think, as hot as you are from that little Mexican hottie in your office, you would want to kill as many as you can to get even for never getting some of that."

"Leave her out of this. Let's finish."

"I think we're ready. Want to go back to sleep and finish with Chica Bonita?"

This time Wiltz simply ignored Charlie's vulgar taunts and went and lay down on his bed. He set the alarm on his cell phone, covered himself with the bedspread and closed his eyes.

At first, Wiltz thought he set the alarm wrong. It seemed only moments before, but it was one-thirty. Time to go.

He changed into jeans, a sweatshirt, and grabbed his Army-issue green jacket from the closet. In the kitchen, he rinsed his mouth in the sink and splashed his face. His stomach churned. From an open carton in the refrigerator, he took a long pull of milk, in hope it would settle his churning guts.

Wiltz took a deep breath, turned off the kitchen light and opened the garage door. The red plastic gas cans waited next to the car. The idea of taking two containers was a bit unsettling, but this was the biggest target. He put them carefully in the back seat.

As he drove once again to Little Saigon, he reviewed the plan over and over in his head. He tried to picture each floor and how many steps it would be to the utility closets. Everything must go as planned.

This was to be the biggest and last fire for Wiltz. He drove past the site several times. He parked and walked the route he would take. On his last reconnaissance mission, he entered the building and took the elevator to the top. He opened the doors on every floor, and when he didn't see anyone, got out. He found a utility closet on each floor he explored. It would follow; such closets would be on the other floors as well. Lots of flammables, wires, and cables he would use them as his kindling.

The building was old, the multiple layers of paint everywhere told the story of its age. He used his pocket knife to help a peeling section of paint come off in a chunk the size of a dollar bill. The top layer was latex, but the five or six layers below were hiding a variety of volatile pigments. It will make great fuel, Wiltz decided.

With Charlie's insistence, it was decided to take two containers of accelerant. Once again, Wiltz added Styrofoam to the mix of one canister to assure it would adhere to the surface he splashed it on. The other was straight gasoline. In his research, Wilt found that gasoline burns at essentially the same temperature as wood, except faster. It has worked in the past; this building would be no different.

Whoever said, "Act like you know what you're doing and you can get away with anything," was right. Wiltz passed two people on the sidewalk walking to the apartment building, but neither paid any attention to him or his five-gallon containers.

As planned, Wiltz used the rear entrance to the building. The quiet of the building reassured him. In and out, home and back to bed. This was the end of the war. He was going home. This time not on a medical flight, not padded and bandaged. He was the victor. He would leave, "mission accomplished."

Wiltz rode the elevator to the sixth floor. With a little luck, the fire would take care of the top two stories on its own. He would torch the floors below until he ran out of fuel. He made his way straight to the utility closet. There were two cans of paint. A small mix of tools sat on a shelf. He grabbed a large screwdriver and started popping open paint cans and dumping the contents on the floor of the closet.

Just like the two floors above, the utility closet was just steps from the elevator. Moving quickly and confidently, Wiltz moved to the dark green door. This time, the utility closet was locked. For a moment Wiltz panicked. He took the screwdriver from his pocket and jammed it hard into the door frame at the striker plate and jerked. The hollow-core door buckled just enough for the latch to slip out. The door popped open.

This is too easy, Wiltz thought, very pleased with himself. He quickly surveyed the contents of the little closet. No paint this time, but like the other, it was mostly storage, except for an old mop and bucket. It occurred to Wiltz he could work faster and more efficiently if he didn't just splash gas and gel. He grabbed the mop, removed the cap on the napalm mixture and gave the mop a soaking.

The trail of gel streamed behind the mop like the tail of a comet, over the tops of doors and down walls. Wiltz poured more of his mixture over the mop and attacked the walls and doors on the opposite side of the hall.

As he worked his way down the hall he could hear the thump-thump beat of hip-hop. As the gel trail dissipated, Wiltz decided to light the fire and go to the next floor. His thought came too late. The door of an apartment several doors down opened, thunderous bass-heavy music flooded the hall, and three young Asian teens in full gang attire came into the hall.

"VC! VC!" Charlie Baranski made his presence known for the first time since Wiltz left his house.

The boys spotted Wiltz. He lit a match and touched the wall. The teens began screaming at Wiltz and rushing towards him. He flopped the mop against the flaming wall and ran towards the boys, waving and jabbing the flaming mop at them. They turned and ran back into the apartment. Wiltz ran the flaming gel over the door and around the casing.

He jammed the bundle of fiery mop strings under the doorknob and kicked the end of the handle to where it wedged in the carpet. Wiltz moved quickly for his gas cans, lighting and touching matches to the gel along the wall as he went.

The thump of the music stopped. The sound of screaming filled the hall. Two apartment doors opened and an old Asian woman peeked into the hall. There was a loud bang. At first, Wiltz thought he was imagining it, but he knew the second blast was a shot fired through the door.

"Saddle up! Incoming enemy fire! Those Zipperheads have us outnumbered!" Charlie screamed. "Now, soldier!"

Without a thought, Wiltz yelled, "Yes, sir!" He grabbed the canisters and ran.

Wiltz frantically pushed the elevator down button. The flames were finding their way up the walls, under doors, along the carpet, and lapped their way to the ceiling. The sound of the screaming gang of teens was rousing more people in the surrounding apartments.

There was no time to wait. Wiltz ran for the stairs. The stairwell was filling with smoke and as he looked over the side he could see the yellow glow of the fire from the two floors above him.

They would expect him to go down the stairs. He decided his only option would be to go up. The smoke and heat increased as he hit the landing on the fifth floor. He couldn't finish the job now. He poured the contents of the napalm canister down the stairwell.

It a moment of bravado, Wiltz dropped a match into the container at the same moment he dropped it. Several floors below, it exploded like a bomb, spraying flaming balls of gel against the stairs and igniting the floor below.

With the partially full gas can in hand, he started up the stairs. The smoke and heat intensified with every step. The deafening bell of the fire alarm screamed through the stairwell. The fire department wouldn't be far behind. Maybe up was not such a good idea, Wiltz thought.

*　*　*

"Breathe, fool!" Charlie screamed.

Wiltz gasped and coughed in the smoky air.

In a hard, metallic clang, the door of the stairwell burst open. The door banged hard against the wall. They were just behind him. Grabbing the gas can, Wiltz ran up the next flight, and this time he didn't stop on the landing. For a split second, he glanced down the spiral opening of the stairs.

Wiltz's breathing was nothing more than gasps. As he started up the stairs he unscrewed the cap on the gas can. There was no choice but to press on.

"Faster!" Charlie's voice seemed to echo in the cavernous shaft.

Ahead Wiltz saw a fire extinguisher hanging on the wall. The smell of gas wafted around him as he ran. He knew what he must do. Setting the gas can down, he grabbed the red canister from the wall and hurled it down the stairwell at the boys. It bounced hard against the rail and struck a boy hard across the head in the middle of the group.

For a moment the pack stopped and tried to understand what just happened to their comrade. It was all the time Wiltz needed. He backed down a few steps and poured gas down the stairwell onto the boys. Without hesitation, he lit his entire box of matches on fire. With a sideward fling of his arm, he threw the fireball at the boys.

His aim was true. The gas ignited, sending three of the boys up in flames. The residue of the gas ignited and set the stairs and stairwell alight. The gang panicked. Some ran back down the stairs. Others began trying to stomp out the flames at their feet.

The boy that caught the bulk of the fuel waved his arms frantically. With fiery hands, he slapped futilely at his face and hair. Then he paused. In a single motion, he threw himself over the rail and plunged the six floors to the checkerboard tile floor below.

The mayhem was enough for Wiltz to run unnoticed to the top floor and the door to the roof. There was still gas in the can, not much, but enough to douse a pile of tarps and a pile of trash left from a repair job of some kind. As Wiltz poured the last few drops of gas on the scraps of plywood and two-by-fours, he looked out over the city.

"I will miss you," he said softly.

As he reached in his pocket he realized he threw his matches at the boys. There was no time. In the distance, he heard sirens. He couldn't tell if it was headed his way or not, but he needed to get away. The first fires must be roaring by now. He must get away.

Wiltz moved to the edge of the roof. The building next door was built without space between. It was shorter than the apartments and dropped at least fifteen feet. The sirens were getting louder; they were coming his way. He must jump.

"Do it," Charlie whispered.

Wiltz stood tall and turned away from the edge of the building.

"Charlie, I have done as you asked. You said this is the last attack. I am holding you to your word as a soldier."

"There is more to do." Charlie's voice was firm and demanding.

"No! I'm through!" Wiltz matched Charlie's intensity and began moving to the front of the building. "I will stop you and you will not bother me again."

As he looked down at the street, he could see people running from the building. Flames were shooting out of windows below, and the fire trucks were rounding the corner.

"This is the end, Charlie, one way or the other," Wiltz said, stepping onto the ledge.

He waited for a response. There was none.

"Do you hear me?"

The voice he'd grown to despise so much was gone. The flames were brighter, the crowd was clearer. Wiltz could hear the shouts of the firemen and the screams of people from their windows. What he didn't hear was Charlie Baranski. It was over.

Turning from the ledge, Wiltz broke into a run. Without hesitation, he leaped from the apartment building to the roof of the building below. He hit hard and felt a sharp pain in his right ankle as he rolled across the rooftop.

The pain grew sharper when he stood. Limping and wincing, Wiltz approached the grey metal door in the center of the roof. A metallic howl of rusty hinges shot through the night as he pulled the door open.

Inside, the pale yellow bulbs in the hall lit the carpet, badly worn, showing years of stain and neglect. To his left and right were doors with peel-and-stick numbers. It was a hotel of some kind. He made his way along the hall, his ankle throbbed, his face wincing with each step. As he approached the end of the hall, a soda machine hummed and cast a fluorescent flood of light onto a staircase with a dark stained banister.

Wiltz started down the staircase, his back to the banister, his throbbing foot dragging behind. The doors read 701, 702 as he reached the next floor. He looked frantically for an elevator. To his right just ahead he heard the sound of a door opening. A man in a light blue uniform was coming out of a door. As Wiltz approached the man he could see he was quite old. His snowy white hair and beard covered his ebony skin.

As he reached the man, Wiltz dropped to one knee and pretended to tie his shoe.

"Mornin'," the man said.

"Good morning," Wiltz replied.

The man was struggling with a luggage cart stacked with books and magazines. In the other hand, he grasped a large metal lunch pail.

"Let me give you a hand there," Wiltz offered.

As he rose to his feet Wiltz slipped his hand in his pocket, struggling to conceal the pain he was in and palmed several dollar bills. They were neatly folded in two, as was his habit.

"Thank you, I'm havin' a time here," the old man said.

Wiltz took the handle of the cart and spun it around, freeing the back wheel from the door frame. The old man pulled the cart into the hall and Wiltz pulled the door closed behind him. Just like when he was a kid in school, he wedged the bills between the door and the lock.

"There you go," Wiltz said softly.

"God bless you, son," the old man said without looking back and rolled on down the hall.

The throbbing in Wiltz's ankle was getting worse and he could no longer put his weight on it. He leaned against the wall, panting with the pain and listening to the thud, thud, thud of the old man and his cart going down the stairs. Several minutes passed and the sound of the descending cart faded away.

Wiltz half-hopped, half-slid his way along the wall until he reached the old man's door. It took no effort to push it open. Wiltz let the bills fall to the floor and hopped inside.

Once inside he felt for a light switch and flicked it on. Across the small room were a bed, a table, and a tattered old easy chair. Slowly and painfully, he made his way across the floor and collapsed into the chair. Wiltz sat with his head back against the chair, his eyes closed.

In the hall, he heard voices, faint at first but growing louder by the second.

"Everybody out! Fire next door! You gotta get out!"

Wiltz froze. The voice grew louder. Heavy knocking now accompanied the yelling. Voices joined in as the moments passed. The door of the small room shook hard from the heavy fist pounding out the alert.

"Fire next door! Everybody out! You gotta get out!"

Wiltz didn't move. Soon he heard the pounding next door. The chaotic sounds of trampling feet and excited, panicked voices died down, then silence. He bent down and untied his shoe and examined his ankle. He knew it would be a bad idea to take his shoe off; he might not be able to get it back on. The swelling around the top of his shoe was severe. It needed to be bound up if he was going to be able to get to his car. The loosening of his shoe helped the pain, but it was still excruciating to put weight on it.

To the left of the chair was the bedroom. Using the wall to support his weight, Wiltz hobbled into the bedroom and to a small dresser. The drawers contained a small assortment of socks and underwear, a few neatly folded sweaters and sweatshirts, but nothing that would help.

The bathroom was only a few steps away. On the counter were assorted toiletries, and an old razor. Wiltz opened one of the two drawers in the cabinet below the sink. Through the pain, he smiled and groaned "Yes" when he saw a half bottle of Sloan's Liniment and an old Ace bandage.

Wiltz unscrewed the cap from the liniment and poured it over his ankle, soaking his sock. He unwound the bandage and poured the rest of the liniment over it. There was not much elasticity left to the old bandage, but he wound it as tight as he possibly could, round and round his ankle. He used the old metal clip to fasten the end and tried to stand.

The pain was less intense. The pressure of the bandage kept it from flexing. Wiltz saw his reflection in the mirror and looked long and hard into his eyes.

"This is almost over," he said and nodded to himself. He reached up and opened the medicine cabinet. Inside, the white metal shelves were rusted all around the edges. A row of amber plastic medicine bottles was the total content of the cabinet. Ernie Johnston was the old man's name, and he took a variety of prescriptions.

The only drug Wiltz recognized was Vicodin. The label warned that the medication was two years past the expiration date. He didn't care. Taking the cap off, he popped three of the pills in his mouth and rinsed them down with water from the sink. All he knew was that he needed to get home.

On the small tidy table in the kitchen was a Bible, a note pad and a pen. As Wiltz passed, he paused and looked at the notes. "My God shall supply all my needs" was written in a shaky hand. Wiltz picked up the pen and wrote.

"Today, He supplied mine. I took your Ace bandage and used up your liniment. Please forgive me. God Bless." He tossed the pen on the table and hobbled to the door.

Although he was an atheist, Wiltz figured this once he could play into the old man's fantasy of a power guiding his life and taking care of him. What else do the elderly have?

The hallway was deserted. He knew the stairs would take him to the main floor and out. The chance of running into someone was too great a risk. Perhaps he would go unnoticed. On the off chance the manager of the building was doing a head check, he would be hard pressed to explain his presence in the building. There must be another way.

At each floor, Wiltz looked for an alternate way to exit the building. Finally, three floors down, he saw a window at the end of the hall. The light from outside seemed to glow orange. The view from the window was the roof of the building next door. From the window, it was almost a direct access. Wiltz unlocked the window and lifted it open. The strong smell of smoke hit him. He put his good foot out the window and climbed out onto the ledge. Along the side of the roof was an access rail. The three-foot gap between the buildings was an easy span to cross. This time Wiltz had no choice but to lead with his injured foot. Little by little, he edged his way along.

There was no way to see how far the ladder ran down between the buildings. Wiltz decided not to chance it and reached for the rusty steel rail. It was wobbly in his hand and he felt unsure of putting his full weight on it. Pushing off with his good leg and using the rail to propel himself forward, Wiltz crossed the divide and landed, tucked and rolled onto the roof.

There was no entrance from the rooftop into the building. From the back side of the building, the alley was lit by the fire of the apartment building beyond. Two fire hoses shot up from the street and were manned by at least seven firemen. Wiltz moved to the side of the building with a view of the street. It was three stories to the street, and at the corner police had it barricaded off. A large crowd gathered to watch Wiltz's final attack. They were getting a good show.

Opposite the old rusty rail, a newer ladder led to the alley space between the building and its neighbor next door. In an effort to save his ankle for the walk to his car, Wiltz hopped and slid down the ladder. Twice he nearly missed the rung and instinctively caught himself with his injured foot. The pain, it seemed, was declining. Either that or the drugs and liniment were kicking in.

As Wiltz neared the bottom of the ladder he could see there was a drop of at least ten feet to the ground. Mustering the last bit of strength in his arms, he did the last five rungs, legs hanging. He guessed the drop to the ground was now a little less than five feet with his arms fully extended. For a long moment, Wiltz hung on the last rung. His head told him to drop, but his fear told him it would hurt his wounded ankle. He knew he should drop, but he just couldn't let go. Finally, his weakened arms made the decision, and he dropped to the concrete below.

To his surprise, he broke his fall with his good leg and rolled to the ground without further injury to his ankle. Wiltz stood, dusted himself off, and made his way to the back alley.

"Hey! Where do you think you're going?" a policeman yelled as Wiltz entered the alley behind the building.

"I just wanted a better look," Wiltz said. His tongue felt thick and his speech seemed slurred.

"Get the hell out of here! What are you, nuts? This is a major blaze. Go on, get out of here!" The policeman began moving toward Wiltz. He couldn't let him near, he would certainly smell the gasoline that splashed on him.

"No problem, officer. No problem. I'm going. I'm going." Wiltz threw his hands up over his head in exaggerated surrender, turned away from the policeman, and moved toward the street beyond.

The inside of Wiltz's car reeked of gasoline. His clothes were soaked. The gas, combined with the liniment, was a heady mix that made him light-headed. The Vicodin dulled his pain and clouded his thoughts. Drive, he thought. Just get home.

Driving was difficult. He used his left foot on the accelerator because his right simply wouldn't bend. It was slow going, but he finally turned onto his street. Wiltz sighed with relief as the garage door rolled up.

He turned the engine off and sat for a long while before hitting the button to close the garage door. He made his way into the house with the single thought of lying down pushing him on.

Wiltz stopped just inside the door. The light was on in the kitchen. He was sure he turned it off. He moved to the living room, the light on the overhead fan was on, a light he never used. The sight in front of him paralyzed Wiltz.

"What are you doing here?"

"Welcome home, sweetheart, where have you been?"

TWELVE

"You need to leave." Wiltz was firm, but he was trying desperately to hide his anger.

"I am home. We will make a home together, you'll see. We can be happy together."

"Terri, I know I upset you," Wiltz was struggling through the Vicodin to find the right words.

The sight of Terri as she sat on his couch in a filmy negligée unnerved Wiltz. He was in a situation that, without the pain and floating effect of the drugs, would have been hard to deal with.

"We can talk about this some other time."

"No need." Terri gave Wiltz a big smile, but there was no joy in her eyes.

"Look, I'm not feeling well," Wiltz offered.

"You do look a mess, sweetie. Let's take a shower and see if we can make you feel all better," Terri said, seductively. She stood and let her thin translucent outer layer drop to the floor, revealing a sheer nightgown.

"No, that's not going to happen. It's time for you to go."

"What is it about me that repulses you so?" Terri growled as she glared at Wiltz. "You are exhibiting very strange behavior lately for a counselor. My counselor is always kind to me. When I tell him about you, he always says, "Just might be the one." She spun so fast it startled Wiltz. "I was looking around, straightening up, you know? I found some curious things."

Terri moved to the end of the couch. She held up two catheter packages and a medical disinfectant pad. "What have we here?" She tossed the items onto the couch. "And what does a man who lives in a townhouse need with so much gasoline?" She bent and picked up a gas can in each hand.

The red plastic containers seemed weightless to Terri as she tossed them on the couch. Wiltz blinked, trying to make sense of what was happening. It was then that he realized they were empty.

"You really do need a shower, darling. Frankly, you reek of gasoline." Terri picked up the funnel and hose Wiltz fashioned before the first fire. "What in the world is this thing?"

"Look, you are a lovely person, quite beautiful, in fact. But you have to realize, I, I, I cannot perform as you would like."

"Of course you can. No need to be shy or nervous because you're out of practice," Terri said re-assuringly.

Wiltz felt a rush of empowerment from the confession. For a moment he was fully lucid. A thought came to him and he acted on it. "Look!" he shouted, as he undid his pants and let them drop to the floor. "Happy now?"

Terri stood motionless, staring at the scars and discoloration of Wiltz's groin. The thin elastic strap around his waist held a clamp tightly against his pelvic muscle below his navel. Fastened to it was the clear plastic tube of a catheter. The tube came from a round plastic stoma in the musculature of the genital wall. There was nothing else there but scars.

"My God, what happened to you?" Terri said in complete shock and revulsion.

"Vietnam! Bombs! War!" Wiltz screamed. "Now will you go?"

Terri walked to where Wiltz stood. Tears were now streaming down his face. She wrapped her arms around his neck. He could feel the softness of her breasts as she pressed against him.

"It doesn't matter. I can't live without you," Terri whispered. "But you have ruined it. You set those fires. I know you did," she whispered hoarsely, as she squeezed him tighter. "They will put you away forever, and I will be alone again."

With a sudden powerful shove, Terri toppled Wiltz. She moved to the couch and felt along the edge of the cushion. Wiltz rolled onto his side, trying to get up. The carpet was wet. He smelled his hand. Gas!

"What have you done?" Wiltz said in horror.

"I found a way for you to be punished, and us to still be together." Terri turned and found what she was looking for.

"This is crazy," Wiltz pleaded.

"You should know, you're the counselor!" Terri chirped sweetly.

"Terri, please. I set the fires. You're right. They had to pay for what they did to me. But you, you haven't done anything. Leave. Call the police if you want. I'm ready to face my punishment. You don't have to do this." Wiltz was on his knees, frantically trying to stand. His injured ankle wouldn't allow it.

"Oh, darling, we are so far beyond that."

Between her fingers, Terri rotated a cheap blue Bic lighter. In one graceful movement, she flicked the lighter and knelt to the floor. The carpet ignited instantly and flames raced across the floor. The couch and curtains erupted in orange flames. Wiltz's gas-soaked clothing went up like a match. He screamed in agony. The last thing Donald Wiltz saw was the pale pink nightgown melt against Terri's skin as she stood motionless before him.

* * *

"Good morning, chief!" Hanna set a steaming mug of mocha before Cole. "That was quite a day yesterday. Tough act to follow."

"Fits and starts, that's the news business. Today will be as dull as dishwater." Cole lifted the mug in a silent toast.

The phone on Hanna's desk began to ring. "So it begins, she smiled.

"I got it," Cole reached for the phone. "Sage."

"Bright and early. Nice to see you back in the groove," said Leonard Chin.

"Oh good, I've been waiting for your call."

"Why?"

"Didn't you get my message?"

"No, I called about the fingerprints on the pipe. They just came back from the lab."

"You got a hit?"

"Yeah, your thumper is a counselor at the VA hospital."

"Donald Wiltz?" Cole said, blowing across the top of his steaming coffee.

"How did you know that?"

"That's why I called you. My guy found him through the records of the Army press office. He was in Vietnam at the same time I worked there. He said I was a condescending smartass in Saigon. Can you imagine?"

"Only the location has changed to protect the innocent," Chin scoffed. "We're going to go pick him up. Do you want to ride along? Pretend you're going to ID your attacker?"

"Yes, sir!"

"Pick you up out front in ten?"

"Great."

"Randy was right!" Cole called through the door.

"Wiltz is the arsonist?" Hanna replied.

"Yes, but how about him pounding on my head?" Cole inquired.

"Does it still hurt?"

"Not really," replied Cole.

"Old news," Hanna said distractedly from the outer office.

"Can't fire her, she makes too good a cup of mocha." Cole took a sip of his mocha and shrugged. "A little sympathy would still be nice."

By the time Lieutenant Leonard Chin picked up Cole at the *Chronicle* building, he already called the VA Hospital to see if Donald Wiltz was in. He was not, Chin was told, and neither was his secretary.

"Looks like we'll be going to the home address," Chin greeted Cole. "He didn't show for work and neither did his secretary."

"Think we got a runner?"

"Could be." Chin hit the lights on his Crown Victoria.

"Thanks for letting me ride along." Cole buckled his seatbelt.

"No problem, I gotta throw you a bone now and then, so when I ask questions you give me a truthful answer." Chin looked straight ahead.

'Like?" Cole figured there was no need to prolong the inevitable.

"How much do you know about the whole Jesse Monday mess?"

"Not much printable. Mostly hearsay, really. I do have a pretty credible witness that believes the whole thing was staged. It's pretty much universally held that Monday's right-hand man, Skeeter Evans, is a force for evil, not the high-minded spiritual message they espouse."

"In English for us poor second-language learners."

"He's behind the whole deal—bribes, staging, and fake news releases. You name it, it was his baby."

"So where is Monday?"

"My best guess? He's in the wind. He reneged on the deal; Skeeter is furious and will go on without him. He's got the money. What is it you always tell me? Follow the money?"

Chin hit the siren and nearly sideswiped a taxi that wasn't pulling over fast enough to suit him. "How much money you figure they have?"

"Hard to tell. It's an all-cash business. Lot of sources and a lot of KFC buckets passed around. Could be substantial."

"And I thought monks were free-loaders," Chin said sarcastically.

The two rode in silence for a while.

"What do you have for back-up?" Cole asked.

"What, badass Sage scared?"

"We are dealing with someone who has obviously had a psychotic break. No telling what he's capable of."

"I've got two cruisers on their way. No lights or sirens. I told them to stay back until we make contact. Geez, Cole, you think this is my first rodeo?"

"I heard the guy talk. Eight on a ten scale for delusional."

"What have we here?" Chin interrupted.

As they turned the corner onto Wiltz's street, the area was cordoned off and there were three fire trucks and several black-and-whites. A building to the left of them was heavily fire-damaged.

"You've got to be kidding me," Chin said, leaning over his steering wheel as he approached a uniformed officer.

"Morning, Lieutenant."

"What the hell is all this?"

"House fire. Called in around two-thirty. Been out for several hours but the coroner, fire inspector, and Homicide are taking a close look."

"Got a name?"

"No, sir."

"Is it 1218?" Chin asked.

"I believe that would be correct, sir."

"You believe this?" Chin said to Cole.

"Live by the sword?" Cole said.

"Got a spot for me?" Chin asked the patrolman.

"To the right, in front of the Chief's car, I think there is room." The officer moved the barricade and Chin drove through.

"No questions, if you please."

"Got it," Cole said.

From the middle of the street where they stood, Cole could see the fire did a lot of interior damage, but structurally, it still looks sound.

"Looks like they got here pretty quick," Cole observed.

"Yeah, the top floor is still in pretty good shape."

A graying man with a brush cut approached the pair.

"Hey, Len, what brings you here?"

"I thought I was going to make an arrest."

"No shit? What charges?"

"Arson," Chin said, not wanting to play up the irony.

"You're kidding? That's..."

"Yeah, I know. So who's in charge?"

"Hearns. He'll be thrilled to see you. Fire's aren't his thing."

"Thanks, Sal."

"No problem."

Water and hoses still covered the street. Several firefighters stood around a large truck drinking coffee. Their yellow fire suits were covered in soot. There was a calm over the scene, and most of the crew were either silent or chatting in lowered voices.

Chin and Cole crossed the driveway to the front walk. The front window blew glass all over the small patch of grass in front of the townhouse. Through the window, three men could be seen in the bright rays of the morning sun.

"Dean, you in here?" Chin called ahead, knowing full well Dean Hearns was in the house.

"Back here," came the reply.

"Chin, what are you doing here?" Hearns asked as they made their way across the soggy remnants of carpet to the kitchen area.

"I thought I was going to make an arrest."

"And him?"

"He thought he was going to make the ID."

"That'll take dental records, I'm afraid. You got an open file on this?"

"'Fraid so."

"Then it's all yours, my friend."

"Gents, I think you know Lieutenant Leonard Chin, and his evil twin, Cole Sage," Hearns said, doing the introductions.

"Good morning," the coroner and fire captain said almost in unison.

"Can we take a look at what you've got?"

The four men went across the small dining area to what was the living room.

"Hope you have a strong stomach, Mr. Sage." The fire captain's comment gave Cole a strong sense of *déjà vu*.

The living room was like a surreal charcoal sketch. The room was awash in light from the sliding door. Shade upon shade of black and gray nearly hid the focus of the investigation, the two bodies.

For a long moment, Leonard Chin stood taking in the scene. Cole's eyes were drawn to the carbon mass near the center of the floor. Obviously, a human form, but the extent of the fire's destruction was unlike anything in Cole's experience. If it was indeed Donald Wiltz, he bore an eerie resemblance to the lava-covered victims of the Pompeii volcano, except black as coal. One hand seemed to be reaching out. The body that the coroner would confirm was a woman seemed to have fallen straight back against the couch, rigid, like a statue of charcoal fallen from its stand.

"Can you walk us through the scene?" Chin asked the fire captain.

"The room was literally soaked in accelerant, probably gasoline. From the looks of it, the point of ignition was near the woman's feet. See the circle there," he indicated a bare spot the size of a pie tin burned through to the cement below. "We found the metal top of a lighter. So the fuel in the lighter combined with the gas burned hot enough just long enough to create that pattern. The two masses on what's left of the couch are gas cans. They burn differently than regular polyethylene. All this will have to be verified by the lab, but I'll bet a month of Krispy Kremes I'm right."

The fire chief moved to the end of the couch. "Take a look at this. It appears the woman was wearing little, if anything. There is no underwire or clasps from a bra, no zippers, just this thin film melted to her. I'm betting a very thin nightgown." He flicked at the material with the tip of a pen.

"Why is she stiff like that?" Chin asked.

"That's the weird part. Look at him. On the floor, reaching, stretching out, toward the woman, if you will. Yet she is, pardon the pun, stiff as a board. It's like she stood for quite a while and burned before falling over. Damnedest thing I've ever seen."

"Can you do a tox-screen on someone this far gone?" Chin asked the Coroner.

"Believe it or not, the chest and thoracic area are still in pretty good shape, enough I'm sure, to get at least a partial on stomach content, maybe even a liver sample."

"Can we get upstairs?"

"I can save you some time. There is one bedroom with a connected bath. No clothes, no decorations, no toiletries, looks totally unused. This one down here appears to have been occupied by whoever lived here, we are assuming the man at this point. You're welcome to take a look. We're pretty much wrapped up here. Since it is a murder-suicide, dual suicide, or whatever, we will need your OK to remove the bodies."

"Did you get plenty of pictures?" Chin asked.

"Tons."

"I'm good, just send me what you got. Chief, are you satisfied there was no outside help on this mess?" Chin queried.

"No, she lit the fire and that poor sucker couldn't get out. Way too much accelerant. It burned hot as hell, for a minute or two, blew out the window, and the fire retardant in the carpet, drapes, and furnishings kept the fire to a melting smolder until our guys arrived. Eleven minutes from the time of the first call."

"I'll take a peek at the bedroom, but it seems pretty cut and dried what we have here. She torched the place and he paid the price." Chin turned toward the bedroom. "Got any questions? You'll be the one with the first shot at this," Chin said to Cole.

"Nope, I'm good. Thank you, gentlemen," Cole offered, extending his hand to the chief and then the coroner.

The chief left the room first and called out the front window to his crew, "All right guys, let's clean up, seal up, and get back to the station."

The coroner went outside and brought in two assistants who carried a stretcher with two body bags.

Cole left Chin to search the bedroom and went outside for some fresh air. As he watched the fire crew drain and roll the hoses, he thought of the lives touched by the bodies inside. The woman was a new twist on what Cole thought he understood of the tragic arson fires Donald Wiltz set; two businesses, a temple, and two monks who slept peacefully in a place of worship.

With Wiltz dead, his motivation has died with him. His demons returned by fire, to their place of fire, Cole thought. The scars and memories of that long-ago war still torment the minds and souls of the young men who fought there. And for what?

Cole's memory drifted back nearly forty years to the teeming streets of Saigon. The big story of the day was the bombing of Discotheque à l'American. Three American servicemen and a dozen or more Vietnamese patrons died in a bomb blast that ripped through the crowded nightclub, setting off a devastating fire.

With cameraman in tow, Cole visited the scene. Vietnamese authorities were still hard at work, aided by U.S. Army personnel, trying to identify and sort the charred remains of the dead. It was the first time Cole saw death first-hand. The sickening, sweet aroma seemed to float on the morning air.

Try as he might, Cole was ill-prepared for the sight of bodies, broken in two, and the contents of their abdomens spilling to the ground. He ran to the street and vomited violently against a wall. His war-hardened photographer came out after a few minutes to where Cole leaned.

"I got what I need. Damn, you look like you got more than you need, kid. I'll buy you a drink. Let's go." The photographer turned and started down the street.

But Cole didn't leave. He went back into the building, talked to an MP who was going from body to body of male victims, looking for dog tags.

"I'd rather take a VC bullet," he remarked as he tried to unclasp the chain of a fallen comrade.

"Who'd do such a thing?" Cole's naive question surprised the MP.

"How long you been in-country, man?"

Cole looked at the MP and for the first time realized he was the same age as Cole, maybe younger.

"Two weeks," Cole replied.

"Well, buddy, get used to this kind of shit. It's a regular occurrence around here. Who'd do it? We can start with the busboys and dishwashers, and work our way up; could be the owner, who's gambled off the profits and needs a way out of the rent. Then, of course, it just could be the Viet Cong!" The MP laughed at his joke.

"This poor bastard won't even get a Purple Heart."

*   *   *

Cole returned to the street, his notebook blank. He didn't need notes. The sights and smells of that day still remained as fresh and real as that faraway morning.

"Hey," Chin called, interrupting Cole's thoughts. "It gets worse."

"How?"

"It seems our boy Wiltz set one last fire before he fried." Chin joined Cole on the sidewalk. "You got some more time?"

"Sure, where are we going?"

"An apartment building in Little Saigon. Three floors were taken out, at least eleven dead, maybe more. Get this, he doused three Lil' Sai Dragons with gas and lit them up. What a piece of work this guy was."

The sight of the building taped off greeted Cole and Chin as they pulled up behind the remaining fire trucks.

"Three-alarm," Chin said.

"Right in the center floors, too," Cole added.

The perimeter of the scene was guarded by SFPD. Chin chuckled, pointing to the entrance. "Look who's here."

Dean Hearns looked up just as the two approached.

"More Krispies say this is your guy, too," Hearns offered.

"No doubt," Chin replied. "The last one."

"The dead are mostly old folks that simply didn't hear the alarm or couldn't make it out."

"What about the kids?"

"Found one at the bottom of the stairwell. Must have jumped. He was alive when he hit the floor, we got brains and blood puddled up around his head. One died on the stairs and the other one's got burns on about 99.9 percent of his body. Slim chance he'll make it."

"Any witnesses?" Chin queried.

"Nope. Somehow your guys managed to walk out unnoticed in the commotion. The weird thing is he had to go up. My guess is the Dragons' place was on the last floor he torched. They must have spotted him and he went up the stairwell to the roof. Fire says the gas on the kids came from above, so they must have been chasing him. The damage on their floor was limited. The other Dragons used an extinguisher and an old wall hose to put out the fire in the hallway." Hearns seemed pleased with his summation.

"Doesn't seem we have a lot to do here. I'll do the paperwork," Chin volunteered.

"Serious? You da man, Chin! Box of Krispies for you!"

"If you keep feeding me those doughnuts I'm going to be as fat as a garden Buddha! I'll take the paperwork on a case-TBA-at-a-later-date." Chin didn't do charity.

"You got it, pal!"

"That was easy," Cole said on the way to the car.

"Perps dead, no charges, no case. One line in my report. I'll give old Dean a big fat report when he least expects it." Chin gave a devilish laugh.

Back at the *Chronicle* building, Cole waved Chin good-bye and made his way to the elevator. The first bars of "My Girl" came from Cole's cell phone.

"Good morning!" Cole said cheerfully.

"Good morning to you!"

Cole couldn't help but smile at the sound of Kelly Mitchell's voice. "So how is it to be a house guest?"

"It's nice." Kelly paused. "But weird!" she whispered.

"Jenny snore?" Cole teased.

"Nothing like that. It's just that, I am so used to being by myself. They are so sweet and they wait on me hand and foot, but they treat me like I'm in mourning or shock or something." Kelly giggled. "It's driving me nuts. Can I come and get you and spend some time with you?"

"I do need to go get a rental car. There's my cover story."

"Perfect! What time?"

"Need to see Chuck about my Jesse Monday story. How about we have lunch and I take the rest of the day off?"

"Are you sure? I didn't mean for you to play hooky, I meant like when you get off."

"I love playing hooky with you. We have a lot to catch up on. I want to know all about your houseboat stuff. Insurance? Replacement? Oh, and plans for the weekend."

"Perfect. You buy lunch, I'll buy dinner! I'm dying for Vicoletto's ravioli," Kelly said excitedly.

"Who could say no to you, and ravioli?"

"Mmmwahh!! See you in an hour!" Kelly rang off.

* * *

"I have some news on Jesse Monday. I wanted you to hear it first from me."

"Sit down." Chuck Waddell pointed at a pair of heavy leather chairs in front of his desk.

"Are these new?"

Cole's old friend and boss took a deep breath. "Chris ordered them as a birthday present for me. They were delivered a couple of days ago."

"Happy birthday."

"My birthday is in December."

Cole smiled, thinking about the funny little man with all the delightful quirks, mannerisms, and outlandish surprises. "You gotta love 'em," Cole said with a big smile.

"I did," Chuck said softly. Then he sat a little straighter in his chair and continued, "So what have you got?"

"I wanted to give you the piece on Jesse Monday. There are a few things that turned up that may be kind of disturbing."

"Go on."

"First off, I think Jesse Monday had a lot of good things to say. Sad thing is, he fell victim to his handler, either unknowingly, or just through vanity, let the message become distorted. The focus got shifted from the love of God to the love of him."

"Not like we haven't seen that before," Chuck interjected.

"Exactly. The wrinkle on this one is the shooting. We, I mean, Hanna Day and I, met one of the guys on the ambulance. Nothing on the record, he was scared of retaliation if he talked. He claims he and the driver were paid fifteen grand to drive the ambulance with all communications turned off. They took Jesse as far as a waiting taxi. He hopped out and another guy hopped in. That's who was taken into the hospital. From there, we got nothin'." Cole cleared his throat. "The whole Jesse is god's son, returning messiah, or whatever version you got, was too much for him and he bolted."

"What about the driver?"

"Grabbed the cash, his backpack and the first flight to Europe."

"Hanna who?" Chuck backtracked.

"Hanna Day, she's my new secretary, slash assistant. She's a natural. Writes and does a mean interview. No degree, but a lot sharper than nine-tenths of the kids out of college."

"Huh. She left the building?"

"Yeah, and you're only paying her secretary wages," Cole deflected.

"At least get her a press card and make sure her liability is covered."

"Will do. Thank you." Cole was taken back a bit by Chuck's reaction but would take it and run. "So what the hell do we run on this, anyway?"

"The obit. Let the cops find what they may. Then go for a bigger story."

"What do you really think?" Chuck pressed.

"I think Skeeter Evans, Jesse's manager, confidante, right-hand man, is dangerous. He had the kid in the ambulance scared enough to skip the country. The other one, the one we talked to, was afraid his part in the deal would keep him from going into law enforcement."

"So you're really covering his ass," Chuck said as a way of letting Cole know he was following between the lines.

"A bit. Anyway, I think Skeeter will be his own undoing. My concern is how we portray Jesse Monday. It could have a deep impact on a lot of good people. People who maybe heard the positive stuff and didn't understand where it was leading."

"Like Chris?"

"Like Chris," Cole agreed. "He had a heart of gold. He was raised Catholic and in his way loved God. He wasn't dumb enough to be misled by the claims of deity by a country bumpkin. He would have dropped Jesse sooner rather than later." Cole wasn't really convinced of anything he'd just said. He knew he could help give Chuck closure. It was up to him to decide what he believed would be Chris' final reward.

"Is there anything you've got that we can stuff into the obit to make it front-page-worthy?" Chuck scanned the print-out Cole gave him.

"That's kind of what I did. Of course, it's your call how much stays in."

"Sounds good. How are you feeling?" Chuck was finished with the Jesse story. "They told me what happened when I got back in this morning. You OK?"

"Fine. How was your conference?"

"It was a conference. Now I have all this," Chuck opened his hands, palms out to the stack of folders and message slips on his desk. "Three days away and somehow I've got *ten* to catch up on." Chuck chuckled goodheartedly. "Thanks, Cole, I think you know what this means to me."

Cole stood, gave his old friend a smile, and said, "I know. I hope it helps."

Immediately after leaving Chuck Waddell's office, Cole went straight to Human Resources for Hanna's increased insurance coverage and to security to get her a press pass. It took a few minutes to get her staff photo embossed on the pass, but Cole insisted he'd wait.

* * *

"Hey, did I miss anything?"

"Haven't you had enough for one week?" Hanna asked.

Cole laid the press pass on Hanna's desk in front of her. "I picked up a little something for you."

"Oh, my." Hanna put her hand over her mouth. She looked up at Cole, tears flooding her eyes.

"With all rights and responsibilities." Cole smiled.

"I don't know what to say."

"What a delightful change."

"Thank you, Cole."

"I wish I could take the credit, but when I told Chuck Waddell what a great job you did, he told me to go get you your own official get-out-of-jail card."

"Still, you told him, and I am so grateful."

"You are still my secretary, first and foremost. No running out to get a hot scoop!"

"Yes, sir."

Cole beamed as he went into his office, but he didn't let Hanna see it.

* * *

The obituary and follow-up news piece for Jesse Monday ran the next day, above the fold, and on the right side, along with a picture from "The Great Golden Gate Park Rally." The man in the picture looked nothing like the one Cole met on the bench at Pier 39. He was more youthful and seemed to glow in the confidence of his message. The suggestion that Jesse Monday was just another in a long line of spiritual leaders that have passed through the San Francisco scene was met with a rash of angry calls and even a few death threats.

The death threats came as a bit of a shock to Hanna, as did the "with Hanna Day" partial byline Cole graciously gave her on the piece. It took a bit of convincing, but he was able to assure her that it was all part of the game and that no escort would be required after work to get her safely to her car.

The story of Donald Wiltz didn't fare so well. It was relegated to the front page of the local news below the fold. The police deemed the fire a murder-suicide and inferred that Terri was somehow complacent in the fires. For Cole's part, he was glad it was Saturday. Hanna would still be walking three feet off the ground when she returned to work on Monday.

Cole put his feet up on the hassock and fumbled in the cracks of the couch for the TV remote. His bowl of double-chocolate brownie ice cream balanced on his lap and he clicked on the TV. He sighed deeply and took a large spoon of ice cream. "Mmmm, I needed this."

THIRTEEN

The front page of *The Chronicle* led off, below the fold, with Cole's story on the life, death, and disappearance of Jesse Monday. True to his word, there was no hint that the "New Messiah" had not died, no mention of their meeting and Cole's counsel to "just disappear." It was true and accurate, fair and non-judgmental. Jesse Monday was a great teacher who succumbed to his handlers and fell victim to believing the hype they created. In the end, he was a mere mortal, and like many before him, and surely many to follow, his desire to become deity was his downfall.

Cole felt a peace in knowing that it was Jesse himself who pulled the plug. Cole felt solace in knowing the old proverb, "Train up a child in the way he should go, and when he is old he will not depart from it." In the end, he knew that was what saved Jesse Monday. Cole breathed a prayer and wished him well.

The article on Don Wiltz, *Little Saigon Arsonist Dies in Fire*, spoke of the multiple fires, Wiltz's time with the Veteran's Administration, but there was no mention of Charles Baranski's suicide as a possible trigger for Wiltz's mental break, nor did it mention his attack on Cole. Don Wiltz was portrayed as another mentally ill vet who abandoned his better angels to lash out at an imagined enemy and bring death and destruction to the innocent.

Skeeter organized a city-wide event in Los Angeles for Easter Sunday. Billboards, bus signs and benches, radio and TV spots boasted "The Birth of a New You and a New City!" The inner circle of the faithful from the Bay Area were transported to help coordinate the event. The death and subsequent disappearance of Jesse Monday were enough to get Skeeter on all the local morning news shows the week leading up to Easter.

The focus was still Jesse, and Skeeter's resentment was barely contained. On KTLA, he fired back at the morning anchor when asked if he thought he was the man to fill the shoes of the "Anointed One."

"I am an apostle! Like Paul of old! I am the new voice of Jesse Monday. He will return in power and glory as a precursor to the return of Christ. They are brothers and will co-reign on the right and left of the Father. Open your eyes!" Skeeter's unyielding, wild-eyed response was played again and again. The clip went viral on social media and it did not convey much love or "truth".

A large part of the Jesse Monday treasury was spent to rent the Staples Center. Security was hired, lights and sound were provided by Universal Sound, and the faithful managed the volunteers gathered to act as ushers.

As Cole sat in church on Easter Sunday with Erin, Ben, and Kelly, three hundred and eighty miles south, the eighteen thousand seats of the Staple Center in Los Angeles were nearly empty. As Skeeter gazed from behind the backstage curtain at the four or five hundred or so seated on the floor in front of the stage, he flew into a rage. He refused to speak and paced the dressing room, alternating between screaming at Jesse for abandoning him and cursing the loss of the treasury on an empty arena. Efforts to console him were met with screaming accusations of "selling out to the media" and "no faith to begin with."

Within an hour, the entire inner circle left the building. One old woman sat motionless on the second row, and finally was awakened and asked to leave by one of the custodians. It would be several hours before Skeeter would be found near the loading dock, hanging from an electrical cord.

* * *

On the back row of a small Apostolic Faith Church on Easter morning sat Jesse Monday. Having no passport, Neah Bay, Washington, on the Makah Indian Reservation was just about as far away as he could get without crossing a border. He sat, head bowed and eyes closed. He let the old familiar hymns of his childhood wash over him like warm, heavenly rain. He hummed and sang softly. He begged God to forgive him. He repented. Not just for his sins, but for his deceit and claims of deity. The ceiling felt like iron, and his prayers seemed to bounce back at him.

The eight members of the choir filed down from the platform and took their seats with their friends and family, nearly filling the forty seats in the tiny church. Henry Kallappa, the lay pastor of the thirty-five-member church, came to the platform.

"Thank you, choir," the man in the black suit and white shirt offered. "He is risen!" Kallappa called out to the congregation.

"He is risen, indeed!" they responded. Jesse didn't look up.

The tie Kallappa wore seemed to choke him. He reached up and loosened his tie and unbuttoned his top button. "You all saw me dressed up. No need to pretend I like it."

His comment was met with laughter. "We are here to celebrate the most important event in human history. The day that death was conquered and the sins of the world were forgiven. You all know me. I was a sinner, a bad man, a bad husband, a bad father, a bad son, and a disgrace to my tribe. Some of you I haven't seen here since Christmas." The congregation snickered and lots of ribs were elbowed. "In a town of eight hundred everybody knows everybody's business. So don't think we don't know. What I was, fits a lot of you just as good. That can change. I changed. God changed me and He can change you. I'm not going to stand up here for my usual sermon time.

"No need to pretend everything's OK. It's not. Dope and liquor are killing our people and it is killing some of you. Some of you are tweaking as you sit here. As a matter of fact, you can hardly sit here. Doesn't mean we don't love you, it means the devil has a hold of you and only God can free your mind and body. We can help. Everybody stand to your feet who are ready and willing to help those in need!"

All but five of the congregants stood.

"OK, you can sit down. God bless you. Now it is your turn. Jesus died so you can live. Don't give me that 'White Man Jesus' foolishness, either. Jesus wasn't white. Don't give me no, 'I'll get clean soon.' Soon you will be dead or in jail. You will lose your family, your friends, I mean real friends, and your mind. You need to get right with God today.

"We all got a fine dinner at home. But like the Bible says, 'Man cannot live on groceries alone.' Well, it says bread, but you know what I mean. There are other needs here today. I don't know what you need but you do. You know. Let me pray with you."

Henry Kallappa stood looking into the faces of the people before him. The silence seemed to take on a sound of its own. After a few moments, without instruction or direction from Henry, all over the small room people began to softly pray aloud.

A rail-thin man and his wife stood. The ravages of methamphetamines were apparent. They slowly walked to the front, hand in hand. A moment later, Jesse Monday stood and started for the back door.

"I wouldn't do that, son."

Jesse turned and looked into the eyes of Henry Kallappa. "You know what you need to do."

Without taking his eyes from Henry's gaze, Jesse made his way to the front of the tiny church.

Many tears later, Jesse Monday stood from where he knelt, born again. Not just in a spiritual sense.

When Henry Kallappa asked what his name was, Jesse replied, "Luke Sage."

"You afraid of hard work?"

"No, sir. I could use some."

"You know anything about construction, Luke?"

"From the cradle. My father was a contractor."

"Meet me here in the morning at seven. We got a job starting. I'll give you a shot. Where are you staying?"

The new Luke Sage didn't answer.

"I thought so. All right, you can stay at my place for tonight. This new walk you've begun today, it won't be easy, but God is faithful." Henry patted his new friend on the back. "I got a good feeling about you, son. Real good."

Luke Sage found a friend, a home, and his God again.

*   *   *

The backyard was a Peter Rabbit wonderland of pastel streamers, giant Easter eggs, and brightly colored, mirror-finish pinwheels. The table was set with Erin's floral china and pastel linen napkins. A large glass pitcher of orange juice sat at one end of the table and two bottles of sparkling Cran-Apple cider chilled in an ice bucket at the other. The centerpiece was a bouquet of Peruvian lilies that exploded in reds, yellows, violets and every shade in between.

In front of each place setting, Jenny carefully positioned a handmade place card with her personalized decoration and each person's name. A stethoscope circled Ben's name, Erin's name was nearly buried in flowers, Kelly's had "grandma" printed over a pair of red lips, Cole was pictured in stick figure flying a kite, and Jenny portrayed herself with the ears and whiskers of a bunny.

On each plate sat a fancy decorated egg; some small, like Jenny's, and some large and decorated in rhinestones and ribbon. As Erin called everyone to the table, and with Ben and Kelly's help, she placed several dishes of food on the table.

"Did everybody find their place card?" Erin asked, as she dramatically stretched and looked around the table.

"I found mine!" Ben said, smiling at Jenny.

Cole walked all the way around the table, then said to Jenny, "I can't find mine."

"Oh, grandpa! It's right here! Grandma, you sit here across from him!" Jenny giggled with delight.

"Are my lips really that red?" Kelly inquired.

"Yes!" everyone said in unison.

Everyone joined hands, and Ben asked the blessing.

"Before we eat, I have a special Easter surprise for everyone. We'll go from the youngest to the oldest. Just like at Christmas. Jenny, you're first!" Erin glanced around the table, then said, "Dad, no cheat-ing!"

Jenny twisted, pulled and popped open her egg. Out fell a plateful of peanut M&Ms. "My favorite!" she squealed.

"They are for after lunch," Erin said firmly. "Let's see how many you can get back in the egg."

"OK. Just one?" Jenny pleaded.

"Just one," Ben answered. "Your turn." Ben smiled at Erin.

"Very funny. Mine's empty. I just set it there to complete the table."

"Really?"

Erin popped open the egg and exposed a rolled-up piece of paper. "What have we here?" Her face beamed as she unrolled the paper and read, "A get-away visit to Casa Esimo Day Spa! Oh, thank you, sweetie." She leaned over and kissed Ben on the cheek. "Your turn."

The sound of the egg breaking brought a grim-ace to Ben as he pulled the lid off his egg. Inside was a brand new watch.

"I thought it was about time to retire your old one." Erin offered.

"I love it. Thank you."

"Grandpa, your turn!" Jenny seemed to bounce with excitement.

"Thanks a lot!" Kelly said in mock offense. "Go ahead, age before beauty!"

Cole picked up the egg and gave it a quick twist. The lid popped off and he reached into the egg and pulled out a tiny pair of blue baby booties.

No one at the table made a sound. Then Jenny squealed, "I'm going to have a little brother!"

Spinning in her chair, Kelly threw her arms around Erin. "Congratulations, how exciting!"

"This *is* an Easter blessing," Cole said, giving Ben a big smile.

The excited chatter of due dates, the baby's room, and names went on for several minutes. In the ensuing excitement, Ben scooped up a big spoonful of fruit salad. Cole poured a glass of orange juice and nibbled on a piece of bagel. Jenny wiggled in her chair and was growing increasingly impatient with her mother and grandmother's chatter.

"Mommy, I'm hungry. Mom-mom..." Jenny whined.

"You're right, sweetie. We can talk about your baby brother for the next six months before we meet him." Kelly's voice was soft and loving.

"Grandma, you still have your egg!"

"Well, so I have!" Kelly said brightly.

To make sure that her appreciation was truly expressed, it was Kelly's ritual of beginning the un-wrapping or opening of every gift with oohs and aahs over the paper, ribbon, or in this case, the beautiful reproduction Fabergé egg.

"This is so precious. Do I get to keep it?"

"If you want, or we can fill it again next year."

Erin looked at Cole and smiled lovingly.

Kelly opened the egg and gazed down with a quizzical look. She looked up at Cole, her eyes flooding with tears. Turning slowly, her eyes met Ben's, then Erin's.

"Kelly, since I met you my life has changed in so many ways," Cole began. "You are a woman who is so secure and sure of who she is that it inspires everyone lucky enough to meet you. I can't imagine my life without you. You are the perfect mother, grandmother, and my reason to be the best me I can be. Your faith and dedication to God make me see the purpose in life I never dreamed was possible."

Kelly sat with her hand over her mouth, tears streaming down her cheeks.

"Easter is a time of rejoicing. Spring is a time of rebirth. A new life is coming to our family. It is also a time when you have lost everything. I want to give you my everything. Will you marry me and make this circle complete?"

"You are my everything," Kelly said tearfully.

"Is that a yes?" Cole grinned.

"Yes, yes, yes!" Kelly took a glimmering diamond ring from the egg and handed it to Cole. "Will you do the honors?"

Cole stood, then knelt beside Kelly. He slipped the ring on her finger and kissed her hand gently.

The next moment they both stood. They kissed and held each other in a long embrace.

"I love you all so very much," Kelly turned to face her son and his family. "And Cole makes my life complete." She held her hand out, showing off her ring. "This is a pretty nice surprise, huh?"

Erin and Ben clapped enthusiastically.

"What do you think, sweetheart?" Cole eagerly asked Jenny.

"I'm still hungry," Jenny said softly.

"Well, there you are." Cole shrugged and gave a sheepish grin. "Let's eat."

THE END

HEART OF COLE

Exclusive sample from Book 7

ONE

"All my friends are dead or have moved away," the old lady said mournfully into her flip phone.

There were only a scattering of people in the park. A man in a pale green warm-up suit was walking a dachshund that insisted on stopping at every tree for a sniff. The old lady frowned as the dog relieved himself against a Poplar.

"I know Atlanta's a long way from San Francisco."

The bench down the walk was occupied by a sleeping homeless man, wrapped, mummy-like, in black plastic garbage bags. His gravely snoring was punctuated by gasps and sputters.

"It has been nearly three years, sweetheart."

Since the old lady arrived in the park, only the occasional bicyclist interrupted the otherwise slow pastoral setting. This was her park. Every morning and sometimes afternoon, she strolled the narrow walkways. It was her habit for over sixty years. As a young woman, she brought her children to run and play. For two brief years, she brought her granddaughter to the park while her daughter finished her graduate degree at the University of San Francisco.

"I know, I know, soccer, ballet, I know. If it's important to her, I know, your yoga classes help pay the bills."

Over the years, she saw the park's landscape change. Trees that were old friends, grew sick or tired and broken and were removed. The carefree dancing, singing, hippies of the sixties were replaced by the junkies of the seventies. The emptiness of the eighties brought the death of her husband, her children moving to the far corners of America, and a lot of the people she knew moved to the Central Valley. During the nineties, a flood of "people of color", as they liked to be called, invaded her park. They too have grown old like her, and like her, their children disappeared in the new millennium.

"No, my," the old lady paused, "my money is tied up in CDs, and it is all I have to pay my bills. Social Security is nice, but things are expensive here."

As she approached her eighty-second birthday, she ached for the days gone by. Sometimes she would look across the grass and see her children running, chasing a ball, or making bubbles with dish soap and plastic hoops—a good life. Now, it seemed a slowly repeating cycle of morning coffee, dressing, not remembering what she wore the day before, walking to the park, soup and half a sandwich for lunch, a nap, the five o'clock news, toast and a bit of jam and a hot cup of cocoa in the evening, an old movie on TV, waking to find the movie over, and going to bed, only to repeat the process the next day.

"What if I came to Atlanta? Are things cheaper there? No, I know you don't have room for me, I know your house only has five bedrooms."

The weekly call from her son in Atlanta was more drudgery than pleasure. She tired quickly of his litany of complaints about his, job, wife and kids. Too little money, too much work, too many demands, and she rarely got a word in. *Perhaps she coddled him,* she wonders. *At least he calls. Something his sister hasn't done in two years.*

"Uh huh," the old woman responded but no longer listening.

Across the park, a black dog attempted to join the dachshund, but was met with snarls and barks from the dachshund, and a series of yelling curses from the dog's owner. The old woman was so distracted by the dogs she didn't notice the person who approached the bench.

"Mind if I sit down?"

The old lady smiled and motioned to the stranger to be seated on her right. She wasn't afraid of people; she loved to talk. The bum in the plastic ensemble, on the other hand, should have been shooed away.

"Alright, I've got to run, too." The old woman snapped her phone shut.

"I haven't seen one of those in a while," the visitor said, pointing at the flip phone.

"I take a lot of ribbing about it." The old woman held up the phone. "But if it ain't broke…"

"…why fix it." Her guest finished her sentence.

The two strangers sat on the bench and watched the man with the dachshund leave the park. No words were exchanged for a long time; they just sat in the morning sun.

The silence was broken when the stranger spoke. "What's your greatest regret?"

The old woman turned and looked at the stranger for a long moment. "Having children. Shocking thing for a mother to say, isn't it? But, I must have done something wrong somewhere. They turned out totally self-absorbed, selfish shits." The old woman chuckled.

"I've heard that before. So what's your greatest joy?" the visitor asked.

"You're a funny one," she said. "Let's see. I would have to say marrying my husband. We had a wonderful life. He's been gone almost forty years now and I still miss him. It hurts like a toothache in my soul."

The new friend looked at the old woman for a long moment, and then asked, "Are you a religious woman?"

"I like to think I know where I'm going when I die."

"So…you're ready to go?"

"You know the old story about the bus to heaven?" The old woman smiled with the anticipation of telling a story to a good listener.

"No, I don't think so."

"I'm not really good with stories but, a preacher once gave a rousing sermon and as he closed, he said with real dramatic flair, 'The bus to heaven is waiting at the front door!' But, nobody went to get on."

"I don't get it." The stranger frowned.

"Nobody is really ever ready to die, are they?"

"I guess not."

"So, what is *your* greatest regret?" the old lady said cheerfully, fully enjoying the conversation.

"That you have to die."

At that moment the stranger's left arm flew across at the old woman. A faint flash of metal glimmered a second before an ice pick was driven deep into her heart.

The old woman's last act on earth was a disgusted humph, and a sneer. Her chin went down and gently rested on her chest. The stranger withdrew the five-inch spike and wiped the small amount of blood on the old woman's coat, where it covered her thin thigh.

"I guess you missed the bus," the stranger said.

The stranger reached the sidewalk that ran in front of the park and turned to look back to where the old woman sat. The late morning sun cast a broad swath of light on the bench. The old woman looked as if she were napping in the warmth of the light.

The stranger's blank stare showed no emotion, no sign of satisfaction, no remorse, or conscience at all. The park was the same idyllic scene; there was just one less soul inhabiting it.

Across town in Golden Gate Park, the sun was just as bright, but the atmosphere was completely different. Families picnicked, kids played, lovers strolled, and bicyclist of all styles cruised in the sunshine. The air was clean and the magic that was San Francisco was in full display.

"What a beautiful day."

"What a beautiful girl." Cole Sage replied rolling on his side to face Kelly Mitchell.

A few yards away, their granddaughter Jenny did somersaults down a small grassy knoll. She surrounded herself with a group of children that looked like the cover of a UN pamphlet. Cole watched as Jenny showed and coaxed the other kids into rolling and tumbling down the hill. How could a seven-year-old have leadership skills? He thought. She must get it from her grandmothers.

"Those chocolate chip cookies taste like more."

"Too bad you already ate the last one!"

"Really?"

"About a half hour ago."

"You should have told me."

"Why?"

"So I wouldn't live in anticipation of having another."

"Poor baby," Kelly sympathized.

"You know, we have a pretty wonderful life. I feel such peace. It is all because of you."

"That's sweet, but I think it is the life we have been given. We are so blessed that Erin and Ben found each other. Then *we* found each other. It is pretty amazing when you map it all out."

"Kind of like that old song. Up from the ashes, up from the ashes, grow the roses of success!" Cole sang.

Cole rolled back and looked up at a big polar bear of a white cloud crawling slowly across the sky. So many things in their life could have gone so wrong. Tragedy was averted time and again. Kelly's houseboat burning, Cole being thrown into harm's way too many times—they truly were blessed. Because here they lay, in the soothing spring sun, on a blanket in one of the most beautiful places on earth without a care in the world.

Gratitude was an attribute Cole Sage began to embrace far too late in life. Now it was something to share, encourage, and offer thanks for. The sermon he heard the previous Sunday came to Cole's mind.

"I am not a Bible scholar."

"Where did that come from?" Kelly sat up.

"I was just thinking about the Sunday sermon."

"And?"

"Well, the pastor said Satan accused God of building a wall of blessing around Job so that Job couldn't help but be thankful to God. The devil said God spoiled Job, so of course, he loves God."

"But it wasn't true. God blessed Job because he loved Him and lived a righteous life. A bit different, don't you think?" Kelly studied Cole trying to figure out where this conversation was leading.

"I don't think that spoiling a person necessarily brings gratitude. It's more likely that people who are given everything become self-centered, selfish jerks."

"OK, I guess that's true for the most part."

"I just hope we're not spoiling Jenny." Cole watched the little golden-haired girl leading the play on the hill.

"Wow! Sometimes your thought connections amaze me. No, I don't think we spoil her that way. We don't bury her in gifts. We *do* give her a lot of love and attention. Not the same thing."

"We are pretty blessed. I hope I am not guilty of just thanking God for what He does for me. I wasn't brought up in a church like yours."

"I think you have a huge heart and are seeing God's blessings in your life and you appreciate them."

"You lost your houseboat and everything in it. You didn't complain once. You just went on with life."

"Well, I was plenty angry. I prayed some pretty angry prayers. But, in the end, I was grateful I didn't end up barbecued." Kelly laughed and slapped Cole on the leg. "Come on, that was a good one.

"Did you ever wonder what you would do if you lost everything like Job?"

"*Though he slay me, yet will I trust in Him.* I think that's the lesson to be learned from Job.

"I wonder if I lost you, or Jenny, or Erin, if I would be able to still love God?" Cole lay back and gazed up at the clouds.

"I hope you never have to find out."

About the Author

Micheal Maxwell has traveled the globe on the lookout for strange sights, sounds, and people. His adventures have taken him from the Jungles of Ecuador and the Philippines to the top of the Eiffel Tower and the Golden Gate Bridge, and from the cave dwellings of Native Americans to The Kehlsteinhaus, Hitler's Eagles Nest! He's always looking for a story to tell and interesting people to meet.

Micheal Maxwell was taught the beauty and majesty of the English language by Bob Dylan, Robertson Davies, Charles Dickens, and Leonard Cohen.

Mr. Maxwell has dined with politicians, rock stars and beggars. He has rubbed shoulders with priests and murderers, surgeons and drug dealers, each one giving him a part of themselves that will live again in the pages of his books.

Micheal Maxwell has found a niche in the mystery, suspense, genre with The Cole Sage Series that gives readers an everyman hero, short on vices, long on compassion, and a sense of fair play, and the willingness to risk everything to right wrongs. The Cole Sage Series departs from the usual, heavily sexual, profanity-laced norm and gives readers character-driven stories, with twists, turns, and page-turning plot lines.

Micheal Maxwell writes from a life of love, music, film, and literature. Along with his lovely wife and travel partner, Janet, divide their time between a small town in the Sierra Nevada Mountains of California, and their lake home in Washington State.

Made in the USA
Coppell, TX
06 February 2021

49837307R00166